Matt was driving along at a sedate pace. She was warm and secure in the middle of the back seat, Rob and Will pressed up on either side of her, even the acid smell of vomit coming off Will seeming comfortable and familiar. And there was Alex sitting in front of her, passive, calm, a reassuring air of strength around him, for all the shock of the last thirty minutes.

She smiled, warmed by friendship, by the fact that Matt would give himself up if they wanted him to, and by the fact they'd never let him, and with Matt's offer still hanging in the air she said, 'No, this stays secret for ever, no matter what. Agreed?'

'Agreed,' said the three of them, Rob with a laugh in his voice.

Alex looked at Matt who turned briefly and nodded.

'Agreed,' he said.

They drove on through the empty town centre, a sense between them that things had been resolved. Natalie settled down into the seat, staring at the back of Alex's head, trying to subdue the part of her mind that was still locked stubbornly on to what had happened back there.

Maybe they all felt the same, for all their attempts to immunize themselves against the reality of the accident. They were thinking of that girl lying in the road, wondering whether anyone had found her yet . . .

'Wignall sidesteps hackneyed dialogue and grips the reader with empathy for the guilty of conscience'
Scotsman

Also by Kevin Wignall

People Die

About the author

Kevin Wignall was born in Herentals in Belgium where his father was stationed as a soldier. After spells living in Northern Ireland and Germany, the family settled back in a small town in the west of England where he still lives. He attended the local school and went on to Lancaster University, graduating with a degree in Politics and International Relations. Certain only that he didn't want a regular graduate job after leaving university, he travelled, campaigned and wrote on the environment and taught English as a foreign language. Having always written, it was during his brief stint as an English teacher that he began work on his first novel. *People Die* ('A killer-thriller with humour and heart' *The Face*), is also available from Flame.

Kevin Wignall

Among the Dead

FLAME
Hodder & Stoughton

Copyright © 2002 by Kevin Wignall

First published in Great Britain in 2002 by Hodder and Stoughton
Paperback first published in 2003 by Hodder and Stoughton
A division of Hodder Headline

The right of Kevin Wignall to be identified as the Author of
the Work has been asserted by him in accordance with the
Copyright, Designs and Patents Act 1988.

A Flame paperback

10 9 8 7 6 5 4 3 2 1

A CIP catalogue record for this title
is available from the British Library

ISBN 0 340 79368 6

Typeset in Centaur by Hewer Text Ltd, Edinburgh
Printed and bound in Great Britain by
Mackays of Chatham, Chatham, Kent

Hodder and Stoughton
A division of Hodder Headline
338 Euston Road
London NW1 3BH

For B.J.M. and G.J.M.

As ever, thanks to my agent, Jonny Geller, and my editor, Carolyn Mays. I'm also indebted to the work of Peretz Lavie for guiding me through the world of sleep research.

PART ONE

I

They were parked facing the river, sitting in the dark watching Will heave his guts up over the railing and into the black water below. For five minutes now he'd just been doubled up over the rail, an occasional spasm the only sign he wasn't finished.

Matt wished he was out there with him, in the fresh air, purging himself. Instead he was sitting hemmed in by the steering wheel and his seat-belt and the oppressive silence that had fallen over them in the car. He wanted to get out, wanted to speak, wanted just to do something, but he couldn't.

At last Natalie said, 'You think we should see if he's okay?' Matt had wanted someone to speak but didn't know what to say now in response. The other two didn't say anything either and she let it drop. They all felt bad, numb and nauseous and shell-shocked. If anything, Will was the lucky one, because he was at least turning it into something tangible.

Matt was really beginning to regret that they'd left the scene, and not just because of the girl, but because it wasn't fair for all of them to get dragged into this. They wouldn't see it like that but he would be dragging them in, and it hadn't been their fault. He was the one sitting behind the wheel.

'I should go to the police,' he said, not so much to them as to himself, wanting to hear the words spoken aloud.

He glanced across at Alex in the passenger seat; no response, eyes still fixed on Will, like he was refusing even to consider it. Matt looked at the other two in the rear-view then, squashed together as though Will were still sitting with them. Rob's face looked set and intense but Natalie started to nod and couldn't stop.

Her face was all nervous ticks as she said, 'Yeah, the police, explain everything. I mean, we should go to the police.'

'Excellent idea,' said Rob, an edge of anger and sarcasm creeping into his voice. Matt looked at him in the reflection; he was perfectly still on the surface but he looked full of adrenaline, like someone spoiling for a fight. 'We'll all go to the police, we'll explain everything. They'll probably give us tea and tell us it wasn't our fault.'

'It wasn't our fault,' said Natalie, her tone hopeful rather than insistent, but Rob was having none of it.

'Like anyone cares! I'll tell you this, if we go to the police we can all wave goodbye to our university careers. And if the four of us are lucky we'll get suspended sentences – I mean, all we did was the leave the scene – but, Matt, you'll get jail for sure, because you're the driver and you'll fail the breathalyser.'

'I've had two beers and two vodkas.' Rob was right though, he was the driver, and maybe he would fail a breathalyser.

As if to drive that point home Rob said, 'Two glasses of vodka, not two measures, and yeah, you're a big guy, big metabolism, but do you fancy your chances? Think about it, you're a rich American, studying in Britain, and you just killed a girl while drink-driving. We know the truth, we know you're not drunk, we know she ran out in front of us, but what we know doesn't matter. I can see the headlines; they'll crucify you.'

'Rob's right,' said Natalie, grasping on to a different hope. She was still drunk, not knowing what she wanted. 'After all, it wasn't your fault, and she's dead, so what good does it do? It wasn't our fault but our lives will be ruined.'

Matt just wanted them to stop. He wished he hadn't even said anything, and it infuriated him because everything they were saying made sense but he still felt like he should go to the police, because it was the right thing to do, because a girl was dead and maybe he deserved to be punished for the part he'd played in it.

Alex seemed wrapped up in a meditative calm and Matt turned to him now, hoping he'd find something to say that might at least put things in perspective.

'Alex?'

'She's dead,' he said without a flicker of expression or acknowledgement. Matt was still trying to decipher what he meant but Rob had no doubt as to whose position Alex was backing.

'Exactly, she's dead. It's terrible, and we'll live with it for ever, but it wasn't our fault.'

'So you keep saying, but really, how do we know that?' Matt looked into the rear-view again. Rob didn't answer this time, just stared back, and Matt added, 'I'll go to the police in the morning. I'll have burned off the beers and vodka by then. I'll tell them I was alone in the car, that I felt something collide but I didn't see anyone. I mean, what's the worst they can get me on? Failure to stop at the scene of an accident. I think they'd have problems making that stick. There isn't even any damage to the car for Christ's sake.'

He thought he'd made a pretty good case, the logic falling together as he'd spoken. Natalie responded immediately though, sounding desperate, almost pleading as she said, 'No, Matt, you have to listen to Rob. This will ruin your life. It'll ruin all our lives.'

'It'll ruin our lives anyway.' It was the most Alex had said since it had happened and Matt stared at him, thrown; Alex was the one who stayed calm, who saw a way through things, steered a course. He seemed to come back to himself then, turning to Matt and saying calmly, 'You can't make this better by going to the police. You need to accept that and then decide if you want to go through with it.'

Matt nodded, relieved, and although he was still confused he could see Alex was probably right. Maybe going to the police was just another way of not facing up to it, of making it someone else's responsibility. Maybe.

Will could feel his stomach was empty, that there was nothing left to come up, the last retch still lodged raw and fruitless in his gullet. He stayed leaning over the rail though, finding some comfort in the disorientation, in the dizziness and the black water below, invisible but swiftly moving.

It was the thought of the others watching that made him finally right himself, and he was angry with himself now, embarrassed. He was sick of the fact that it was always him, that he was the one who always managed to drink too much, to screw things up, to fall apart.

They'd be the same as ever, saying it didn't matter and not to worry about it, and they probably had no idea how it made him feel to be constantly patronized like that. They meant well, that was the worst of it, because sometimes he felt like their pet project, like he was the misfit they were trying to rehabilitate.

He turned and sat against the railing for a second or two, wiping his mouth on his handkerchief before looking up at the car. He couldn't see Rob and Natalie in the back but Matt and Alex were visible in the light of the streetlamp. Matt's eyes were downcast but Alex was looking at him and smiled now.

Thank God for Alex. Will smiled back at him and walked slowly to the car, readying himself. He had to make them believe he was okay, that throwing up had been about the drink, not the accident, because it wouldn't take much for them to start worrying about him, that he wouldn't be able to deal with this.

He opened the door and climbed in next to Natalie who said, 'How do you feel?'

'Okay. What's the feeling here?'

Nobody answered at first and he couldn't understand why, thinking it had to be about him, but then Matt said, 'I was thinking about going to the police in the morning and saying I was alone in the car. The others think we should let it be.'

Will nodded, thinking it over. He wanted to go to the police too, but he could see how it would look if he said that, like he was throwing Matt to the wolves.

Matt turned, looking expectant, and Will said, 'What, you want my opinion?' Matt smiled and nodded, like it should have been obvious. Will thought about it. He had to sound like he was holding it together, especially now. He didn't want Matt to go to the police on his own anyway. 'A bad thing happened. Bad things happen. I don't think it was anyone's fault, just circumstances. So we have to ask ourselves how we can extract the most good from this bad situation.'

He'd overdone it, talking about extracting good – what good could come out of something like this? He was bracing himself for some harsh comment to that effect from Rob but he was silent, and Matt sounded regretful but accepting as he said, 'I suppose you're right.'

'Good,' said Alex, as if it were settled. He turned in his seat then and said, 'You realize, though, we all played a part in leaving her, not just Matt, and if we don't go to the police we've broken the law. That means we can never discuss this. It stays among the five of us and goes no further.'

Will nodded, as if Alex were talking to him more than the others but Rob laughed, indignant as he said, 'Alex, I hardly think we need the "secret pact" speech; we've been friends for two and a half years, best friends. I think we can all trust each other without resorting to melodrama.' He was overbearing sometimes but Will couldn't help but admire the way Rob always seemed to find the right words, his fluency. Alex just shook his head though.

'I'm not talking about trusting each other, I'm talking about trusting other people. I'm saying if it gets into the wrong hands this information could hang us all out to dry. So we have to pretend it never happened.'

Will was waiting for another response from Rob but none came. Matt gave a deep sigh and started the car.

'Okay,' he said, 'let's go home.' He backed up and turned carefully into the road, and then as he drove along the quay-side he said, 'Let me say this though. Sleep on it. And if any of you decide in the morning that you can't handle it, then I'll go to the police and tell them I was alone in the car.'

None of them said anything and Will felt comfortable again, for once feeling like maybe he wasn't the weak one, like they were all in this together, equals.

Natalie had been silent now for a few minutes. She'd felt drunk again, her thoughts unclear, and it had been easier just to sit there and listen to the four boys discussing it. She didn't think the conclusion had ever been in doubt anyway and now that it had been decided she felt more relaxed.

Matt was driving along at a sedate pace. She was warm and secure in the middle of the back seat, Rob and Will pressed up on either side of her, even the acid smell of vomit coming off Will seeming comfortable and familiar. And there was Alex sitting in front of her, passive, calm, a reassuring air of strength around him, for all the shock of the last thirty minutes.

She smiled, warmed by friendship, by the fact that Matt would give himself up if they wanted him to, and by the fact they'd never let him, and with Matt's offer still hanging in the air, she said, 'No, this stays secret for ever, no matter what. Agreed?'

'Agreed,' said the three of them, Rob with a laugh in his voice.

Alex looked at Matt who turned briefly and nodded.

'Agreed,' he said.

They drove on through the empty town centre, a sense between them that things had been resolved. Natalie settled down into the seat, staring at the back of Alex's head, trying to subdue the part of her mind that was still locked stubbornly on to what had happened back there.

Maybe they all felt the same, for all their attempts to immunize themselves against the reality of the accident. They were thinking of that girl lying in the road, wondering whether anyone had found her yet, wondering whether she was a student or a local, how it would feel in the morning, in the weeks ahead, the months, just wondering.

She rested her head against Rob's shoulder and closed her eyes, allowed herself to be lulled by the warmth and the engine noise, the movement of the car. She didn't want to think about it. She wanted to pretend it had never happened, as if in the morning it would all be gone.

2

As Natalie surfaced from sleep she was conscious of him moving about the room. The kettle was boiling, a soothing background like distant trains. He was getting mugs out, putting coffee in the cafetière, small domestic sounds that made her feel secure and protected, content.

Alex usually stayed in her room but she liked it when she stayed in his, liked the feeling of being wrapped up in his world, the subtle scent of him in the duvet that enveloped her, the books and photographs and posters that she knew almost as well as her own.

The kettle switched itself off and as he poured the water the smell of the coffee drugged the air, teasing her finally into opening her eyes. He was close enough to reach out and touch, standing there with the coffee things on the desk in front of him.

He had the same look of concentration he always had when he was doing simple things. He'd actually be thinking over some complex problem that was puzzling him but it made him look like a little boy, determined not to mess up whatever task it was he'd been given.

He was dressed, already back from the shower, his hair still wet and looking dark and unkempt. In the summer his hair became almost blond but it was darker now anyway, half the winter already behind them.

Finally he noticed she'd woken and he looked down at her and smiled. She smiled back, involuntarily, like a schoolgirl with a crush, all her love for him welling up. He looked happy too, a glimpse through the baggage and routine and familiarity to what had brought them together in the beginning.

He bent down and kissed her, running his hands through her hair. He smelt fresh and she was full of sleep and in need of a toothbrush but with Alex it was okay, comfortable. She held him tight and he laughed a little, almost pulled off balance.

His cheek was warm against hers, his breath falling hot on her ear. 'Coffee?' he said after a second or two.

'Coffee,' she said and let him go.

She sat up then, his film poster of *They Live By Night* facing her on the wall at the foot of the bed. Alex was wearing a T-shirt but the room was colder than she'd thought and she pulled the duvet up around her neck, carefully sending out one arm to take the mug of coffee from him.

'Thanks.' He sat down on the chair facing her, sitting at a slight angle so that he could put his feet up on the edge of the bed. They both tasted their coffee and then she said, 'You're up early.'

'It's half ten,' he said, but it was clear he knew what she meant: up early for a Saturday, after a night out. 'I couldn't sleep.'

She took the explanation at face value, thinking nothing of it at first, and then without warning the memory of the previous night crashed back through the calm.

'Fuck! I'd forgotten. How could I forget it?' She was reeling. She'd woken up snug and content, and now she felt cold, full of lead, the way she knew she'd feel from now on. 'Sorry,' she said, feeling she'd been insensitive somehow.

'Don't be.' He sipped at his coffee and added, 'I wish we *could* just forget it. I'd love to fall asleep and not think about it.

I couldn't though. I don't think I slept at all.' She pushed her other hand out from under the duvet and rested it on his leg, nodding that she understood, that she felt the same way, and feeling like a fraud all the same because she'd slept well.

They sat in silence for a while, the fractured elements of the memory tumbling back into place. She still couldn't see it from enough distance to make any sense of it. They'd been driving, that girl had virtually thrown herself in front of the car, and she was dead. It was too extreme.

'I can't believe this has happened to us.'

'Nor me.'

He laughed then and she said, 'What?'

'I'm just thinking,' he said. 'What happened last night was horrible. I mean, I haven't stopped thinking about it all night, but it's a bit obscene, isn't it, to talk about it like something bad happened to us?' She nodded, an admission of guilt, but he kept talking. 'You know, we've had a bad experience but that girl's dead. There's a family out there that's probably in freefall right now because of what happened last night, devastated, and they'll never know who did it or how it happened.'

She wanted to feel sorry for this unknown family that Alex was talking about but instead she thought of Matt, wondering what kind of night he'd had, how he was coping. 'It's gonna be tough on Matt too.'

Alex nodded and said, 'That's why we have to stick together. This wasn't his fault.'

The phone rang and Alex jumped up quickly to answer it. He said only a few words – hello, hi, yeah, okay – then put it back down and said, 'It's Rob.'

'Is he coming round?' Alex nodded. 'I'll go and get a shower then.' She got out of bed and felt instantly hung over, realizing for the first time since waking how drunk she'd been the night before. That's why she'd forgotten about it, why she'd slept. She took another mouthful of coffee, pulled her jeans and T-shirt on, picked up her other clothes and her keys, lurching through each movement. 'I won't be long. I'll come back along.'

'Okay.'

She was about to leave but stopped at the door as one of the night's details came back to her, a memory that made her feel sick and giddy.

She'd been sitting in the back between Will and Rob and she'd been cajoling Matt to go faster. He'd ignored her at first but then he'd given in and put his foot down, accelerating quickly. Maybe he'd been going too fast, maybe that had been the cause of it, and if it had then it had been her fault.

She heard Alex say, 'What's up?' She turned and he'd already crossed the room and was standing facing her. He smiled. 'What is it?'

'I just remembered, I told him to go faster.'

Alex's smile grew warmer. He lifted his hand and smoothed her hair, like it was out of place and he was putting it right, his fingers delicate.

'He was doing about thirty before you told him to go faster and about forty afterwards. It wouldn't have made any difference.'

'He was really only doing forty?'

Alex nodded. 'A freak accident, that's all. Nobody's fault.'

She nodded, but was shocked by the thoughts sounding in her own head: relief for herself, but anger too, a feeling that it had been the girl's fault, that she'd done this to them.

'I won't be long.' She kissed him, grateful for his assurances, for being there.

She walked along to her own room then, trying to keep

moving through the hangover. She put all the clothes she'd worn in her laundry bag, even the jeans, put on her bathrobe, picked up her towel and things for the shower, concentrating on the movements, not thinking.

It wasn't until she was under the hot water that she started to piece together her thoughts on what had happened. She was embarrassed now thinking about the way she'd panicked, the things she'd said. She'd been drunk – momentarily jolted sober by the accident, but still drunk.

She remembered she'd wanted to go to the police, then not, a vaguer memory of something about keeping it secret for ever. She was certain the others would remember it too, because they hadn't been as bad as her, and Matt had only had a few drinks.

That made it worse because the more she thought about it she didn't think it was such a good idea to keep it secret anyway. If they kept it secret and then it came out they'd all be in trouble. She didn't want to see Matt get hurt, and it hadn't been his fault, but he'd been the one driving.

She knew what would happen today. Matt would want to go to the police like he'd said, claim he was on his own, the whole story, but then the others would talk him out of it. It just didn't seem fair somehow, that they'd try to keep this secret when it would be better for all of them if they didn't.

The others probably wouldn't care about the consequences either, but it scared her, the thought of having to phone her parents and tell them she'd been thrown out, maybe even prosecuted. And it was even more unfair because all she'd been doing was sitting in the back seat, a passenger. She'd been a bystander and yet this could be left hanging over her head indefinitely.

She'd just turned off the water when she heard the shower-room door open. She pulled back the curtain and saw Sarah Devine putting her towel up on one of the hooks along the bench from where her own things were. Natalie was pretty confident she wouldn't speak.

She turned as Natalie stepped out of the cubicle though, and said, 'Hi, did you hear the news? A student was killed in town last night.' She looked excited, like she'd heard it on the radio and had been itching to tell somebody.

Natalie reached quickly for her towel and held it in front of her, making an appearance of being in a hurry, drying herself as she said, 'Killed how?'

'Hit and run. It didn't give her name, just said she was a student at the university.'

'How awful.' Sarah responded with something or other but Natalie started to dry her hair, obscuring her face, making clear that the conversation was over, and she continued to focus on drying herself until Sarah gave up and got in the shower.

It left Natalie shaken again, not so much the information that the girl had been a student, not even the reality of it being information now, something that was in the public domain. She was concerned about how transparent she'd felt. Maybe Sarah Devine wouldn't have noticed it anyway because Natalie never spoke much to her, but other people would pick up on it, a complicity she felt she wouldn't be able to conceal.

She hurried back to her room and dressed, and as she walked back along the corridor to Alex's room she saw Will approaching from the other direction. He was wrapped up in his coat, scarf, ski hat, his face almost hidden. He looked like he was trying to disappear completely and she felt sorry for him, conscious that he wouldn't be finding this easy either.

She got to the door first but waited for him and when he got there she put her arms round him and held him for a second.

She stood back and looked at his half-hidden face, ruddy, surprisingly healthy-looking. His eyes still had that caught in the headlights stare they often seemed to have.

'How are you feeling?'

'Not good,' he said. She got the feeling he'd have said more but even those two words sounded like they'd stuck in his throat with all that impacted emotion. She smiled at him and pulled his hat off, his hair left unkempt like he'd just fallen out of bed. He managed a smile back and they walked in.

Rob was already in there, talking to Alex. She headed straight for the bed and lay on it. Alex was asking Will if he wanted a coffee, Will replying that he could kill a drink. She only half heard the banter that followed but the end result was Alex reaching for the whisky bottle and lining up the glasses.

'Natalie?'

She looked over and said, 'God, no, not after what I drank last night.'

They bantered on and Alex came and sat next to her on the bed. She wasn't listening to them at first. All she could think about was how this whole group dynamic was beginning to get her down. Will was wired and needed a drink in the middle of the morning, so everyone had to have one, all boys together.

Then she heard Will say, 'I heard it on the radio. She was a student.'

She leaned up on her elbow and said, 'I heard that too. Sarah Devine told me.' She'd known it already and yet it was only hearing Will say it that she became conscious of this being a real person who'd died, a student, someone she could have sat next to in a lecture or encountered in passing around the campus.

Then Will broke the real news. 'They found the body at four o'clock this morning.'

Rob didn't even give it time to sink in, the fact that she'd lain there for nearly two hours, an abrupt dismissal as he said, 'Look, who cares how long she was in the road? She was dead. It made no difference to her.' None of them responded, knowing that it meant nothing anyway, that the bluster was just Rob's way of dealing with things.

Natalie lay back again, staring up at the ceiling, then propping a pillow behind her head so that she was looking at the film poster. With Alex sitting on the bed next to her she couldn't even see Rob or Will and that was how she wanted it for now, to be removed from them.

She didn't even sit up when she heard Will making a nervy suggestion that they should go to the police after all. She listened to Will's case, that it would haunt them, that it would be hard to keep it secret for ever, that it was wrong, but she switched off again as, inevitably, Rob and Alex reassured him and convinced him that they had to stick by Matt.

She studied the film poster, struck by how appropriate it was to their present situation: the car, the tag line, 'we're in a jam', the young couple on the run. She'd never seen the film, had never previously heard of the actors either, but she'd come to love that poster and now it was as if their own lives were mirroring it – except Alex and Natalie weren't just a young couple, but part of a group.

There was a heavy knock at the door and Matt walked in. She could see him as he came through the door, looking in danger of simultaneously hitting the top and sides of the frame. He smiled at her and she smiled back, caught out by his warmth, his openness.

He accepted a drink as he sat down but didn't take any of it before saying, 'Okay, I know we agreed on this last night but, cold light of day and all that, I wanna give you another chance.

I'm more than happy to go to the police on my own. Just give me the word and I'll do it.'

It was as if he were desperate to own up but felt like he couldn't do it without their consent. And she felt sick in her stomach, wanting him to sacrifice himself but knowing she couldn't argue for that, because if she did they'd look at her like she was a traitor. Instead she just lay there listening as Rob and Alex went through the same process of persuasion.

In the end, even Will joined in, no indication at all that he'd been talking about going to the police himself not long before. Will was talking about the flaws of the justice system now and it made her want to scream because he was lying. He was terrified and upset and yet he was pretending he wasn't because he was so desperate to be accepted.

It was crazy, this circular determination to keep everything within the group. It was almost as if they revelled in it and were grateful. They had only a little over a term left together before life took them their separate ways, but now fate had handed them something that would bond them for ever.

That was how they sounded, like they were happy. At least, that was how the three of them sounded. As the conversation continued she noticed she hadn't heard Will say anything for a while, and when he did eventually speak again it was to say he had to go.

She sat up, wanting to hear his explanation.

'Seriously, I have so much stuff that has to be in by next Friday. And I can hardly ask for an extension on the grounds of being involved in a hit and run.'

For an awkward moment their faces were frozen, and then he smiled and they relaxed.

'Sure,' said Alex. 'Well, you know where we are.'

'I'll come over later,' said Rob.

Will nodded but didn't say any more and got up to leave. Natalie wanted to stop him, to hold him again and tell him he was right to be feeling upset and confused. But as much as she was concerned for him, knowing how sensitive he was, she didn't move. She let him go.

When he'd left the other three exchanged glances, as close as they were, the first chink in the group armour. They were worried this would be too much for Will, that he'd go over the edge and start talking. They'd have thought that about him sooner or later anyway but Natalie suspected they still couldn't see the real danger of what they'd done here, a danger to which they were blind because they were too busy focusing on Will.

This bond they'd engaged in so readily was a crime in itself, something that would be as likely to drive them apart as keep them together, making them suspicious, increasingly on their guard with each other. And if their friendship fractured it would stop being a bond altogether, becoming instead a knowledge of the past that could be used to hold each other to ransom. Where would they be then?

Matt looked at the whisky in his glass and put it down without drinking any more of it. 'I'll go after him, just to be on the safe side, make sure he's okay.'

'Sure,' said Alex. 'I'll call you later.'

Matt got up and walked to the door, but stopped then and hesitated. He turned again and said, 'I can't believe I forgot to mention it. Her name was Emily Barratt, a second year in my college. I heard two girls talking about it below my window this morning. She was studying English.'

'It doesn't matter,' said Rob.

'It does.' He was insistent. 'Whether or not we tell the police, it still matters who she was. She was a real person, a human being, and her name was Emily Barratt.' He left, not waiting to see Rob's humble nod to the truth of what Matt had just said.

Natalie lay back again, not listening to the resumed conversation between Rob and Alex. She wanted Rob to leave too, to leave them on their own so they could just be together and deal with it together, her and Alex. She didn't want to be part of a group any more.

She looked up at the poster with its credits running along the bottom – Cathy O'Donnell, Farley Granger, Howard Da Silva – imagining their own names up there instead, and now this newcomer, introducing Emily Barratt as the victim. That wasn't just a name on a film poster though.

Like Matt had said, Emily Barratt was a real person and now she was dead. They'd never known her but their own lives would never be the same as a result. Natalie had no idea how big the difference would be. She hoped against hope that it might be slight, the whole business reduced within months to a distant and unclear memory.

Yet she was full of foreboding, and most of it centred around these people who'd been her friends for the past two and a half years, their weaknesses suddenly apparent. Matt: too noble, desperate to fall on his sword. Rob: too impetuous. Will: too weak and, most of the time, too drunk. All of them were a risk when it came to something as serious as this.

Alex was the only one who was strong, grounded, and maybe because of that she should have been happy to see him with the others, but she wasn't. She wanted to be alone with him, for them to close themselves off from everything outside and pretend like this had never happened. She wanted Alex alone.

3

Will was sitting in the kitchen eating cereal. It was turned nine now and the rush was over. Three or four people had been in and out, none of them saying anything to him. He'd been in the same college with these people for three years, knew their names and who they were. They probably knew who he was too.

But they didn't know each other, and Will was one of those people recognized by everyone as in the college but not of the college. Everyone made choices and that had been his, a good choice too, but this morning he almost wished he'd taken a different path two and a half years before.

And this morning he could have used some idle conversation with these people who lived around him. Instead, he sat over his cereal for forty-five minutes, taking a mouthful, concentrating on it, chewing slowly, taking his time. For a few days now his nerves had been jangling up on themselves and for some reason he found eating cereal relaxing.

He'd finished and was sitting there with the empty bowl in front of him when Lorna came in. He didn't know her either but he knew she studied art and that her name was Lorna. Sometimes when he came in at night or in the early hours her light would still be on and door open but he'd never knocked, never called in.

She was probably attractive but she was some kind of gothic

hippy, hair dyed black, clothes to match – she looked like Morticia Addams. Actually, he quite liked the way she looked but he'd just never had the guts to say so to anyone. He liked that she was willing to look different, stand out.

She did what the others had done, walked in and acted like he wasn't there. He wasn't sure if she'd thrown her eyes upwards at the sight of him. Maybe it bugged her even to have him in the kitchen while she was in there. She went to the fridge and got milk.

She was about to walk out again when Will decided to risk it and speak.

'Hi.' His voice sounded too quiet and he cleared his throat and repeated himself. She'd heard him the first time though. She turned and stood there holding the bottle of milk and looking at him, part quizzical, part hostile.

'Hello,' she said, noncommittal. At least she'd said something. At least she'd acknowledged that he was there. They were the first words the two of them had ever exchanged.

'I'm Will.'

She looked stunned, her face paralysed in surprise for a second before she laughed incredulously and said, 'It's a bit late for introductions, don't you think?' He didn't respond and she gave him a suspicious look and said, 'Let me guess, you've fallen out with your little group of elite friends so you've decided to finally fraternize with the untouchables in your own college. That would explain why you've been hanging around the kitchen the last few days.'

He shook his head. He hadn't fallen out with anybody. It was difficult to be with the others at the moment, the feeling all the time that they were sizing him up, almost as if they were expecting him to crack. But he hadn't fallen out with them, and would never. They'd always stuck by him and he'd do the same.

'I haven't fallen out with anyone. I just . . . I wanted to say hello, that's all.'

She looked at him, puzzled, and then she came and sat across the table from him. She opened the bottle and drank some of the milk, wiping her mouth before saying, 'Okay, I have to say I'm intrigued. So you're Will Shaw and I'm Lorna Pallister, we're both in the same college and the same year. I'm studying art. You're studying God knows what.'

'Politics.'

She frowned, but he could tell it was because she was curious rather than annoyed. He supposed she had a right to be curious, because it was true, he had been aloof for the last couple of years. It hadn't been intentional and they didn't think of themselves as being an elite or anything, but that was probably how it had looked.

He said, 'So what are you doing today?'

The frown was still fixed in place but as if speaking to a young child she said, 'Well, it's a beautiful sunny day, so I'm driving out to Harland Point where I'm going to take some photographs and maybe do some sketching.'

He didn't mind the way she was talking, because beneath the way she looked and the gentle teasing she seemed like a nice person, warm, funny maybe.

'When are you going?'

'As soon as we've finished this little catch-up, which I have a feeling could be quite soon.'

'Could I come?'

'Excuse me?'

'Could I come to Harland Point? With you. I've never been.'

She stared at him, another incredulous laugh.

'This is turning into one seriously weird morning.' Then,

23

like it hardly mattered either way, she said, 'Yeah, you can come. Wrap up warm.' She got up and put the milk back in the fridge.

Will was happy. He hadn't been happy at all in the days since the accident. The closest he'd come had probably been throwing up into the river, the sense of momentary relief that had come with it, the sense too of being lost out there in the darkness with the water moving swiftly below him.

Now he was happy, excited even, just to be escaping with someone he hadn't previously known, to a place he didn't know. The only shadow was the fear of being seen by one of the others. It hardly mattered – they all had other friends – but he still didn't like the idea of being seen because he didn't want them to have any reason to doubt him.

They walked down into the car park and she pointed at a big black Mercedes, old, from the 1950s maybe. He'd seen it there plenty of times but had always imagined it belonging to one of the lecturers.

'This is your car?'

'No, but I found the keys lying around in the bar so I've been using it.' She opened the boot and took the sketch pads and camera case he'd been carrying for her. She looked at him then, misreading his expression. 'I'm joking.'

'I know.'

'Oh.' She opened his door and walked around and got in behind the wheel. 'My dad wanted me to have something sensible and small but I saw this and fell in love with it. He gave in, of course. It didn't cost him much more anyway.' She started it up and pulled out, the car kicking into life as they drove off. 'On the other hand, I can hardly afford to drive it, which also makes him happy.'

Will was looking out at the people they were passing on their way off the campus, studying the faces for anyone familiar. He focused back in on what she'd said then. 'I can give you some money for petrol if you like.'

She laughed. 'I meant I couldn't afford to drive it to London and back once a week. I think Harland Point might be within my reach.' He wasn't sure if he'd offended her but clearly she was thinking along the same lines because she added, 'Thanks though. I appreciate the offer.'

'That's okay. You get on well with your parents?'

'Yeah, they're cool.' That was it, end of subject. He was envious, that someone could sum up her entire relationship with her parents in just three words. 'I'm sorry, was I meant to ask you how you got on with yours?'

'No. I don't do that. I don't like people who ask questions just so that they can answer it about themselves.'

'Nor do I,' said Lorna, not sounding serious and then she laughed again. She laughed a lot for someone who looked that scary. 'So how do you get on with your parents?'

He looked out at the winter sunshine blurring the edges on everything, the sky blue and cloudless. He didn't want to think about his parents, or his whole family with its limitations and suffocating attitude to everything, the way they made everything difficult. This day was too beautiful and he needed its beauty.

'It's not really a good subject for me to talk about. Suffice to say, they'll throw an absolute fucking fit when they come to my graduation. My tutors think I'm heading for a first but seriously, when my parents see me go up there to get my politics degree they will fucking explode.' He laughed at the thought of it, knowing how extreme the reaction would be. 'I'll be cut off, thrown out of the family home, so on and so on.'

She looked away from the road briefly and said, 'Why?'

'Because they think I've been studying law for the last three years. I swapped courses and never told them. And believe me, it says everything you'd need to know about my family that it was easier not to tell them.'

'Jesus!' She looked like she was thinking about it for a few seconds and then she turned briefly again and said, 'Imagine if you'd been gay!'

He laughed, wishing he'd met her earlier, wishing it hadn't taken something bad to show him that there were other people out there. He still didn't regret how close he'd been with the others though, because they'd always been there for him, and they'd had plenty of good times to set against this one tragic moment.

They were driving away from the campus now and he began to relax. He knew about Harland Point, that it was remote, nothing out there, no proper road. He could be out there for a few hours and not have to see anyone or feel under scrutiny.

It was like Lorna had read his thoughts though, because she said, 'So really, what is it with you at the moment? Why suddenly more present in our humdrum little lives?'

'I don't know.' He thought about it, not sure what to say. 'I've just been a little down these last few days, that's all. So . . .'

'Why are you down? Oh, don't tell me. I can guess. In the best tradition of these things, I bet it was your rich little clique that killed that girl the other day, and now you're all overcome with remorse and realizing how shallow and empty your lives have been.' She was facing the road as she talked, a relief because she didn't see his initial shock, and by the time she'd finished he'd realized she was joking, having fun.

He felt jumpy though, like the truth was still on his face, and when she turned for a response he felt like he had to say something that would explain his expression without making him look guilty.

'I don't think you should joke about someone who died.'

'I wasn't joking about her,' said Lorna, making clear that he'd missed the point.

'And you're wrong about my friends.'

'Am I?' He nodded. She seemed to consider it and said flippantly, 'Let me think, there's that girl Natalie. What is she, your mascot? Seriously, what a vapid empty space of a woman. Rob Gibson – completely arrogant wanker. Matt whatever-his-name-is, walks around like he owns the place. Alex Stratton—'

'Alex is okay,' said Will. For some reason he didn't want to hear her run Alex down. She was wrong about the others too but Alex had been a good friend over the last couple of years, the one who'd really cemented him into the group, who'd always been there for him too, a calming influence. If Alex hadn't been there the other night things would have been a lot different, worse. 'Alex is a good person.' He looked at her and said, 'And what about me?'

'I don't know,' she said, implicit in her tone that he was still an unknown quantity, that perhaps she still hadn't come to grips with the fact that he was even in her car. 'You know, I have to admit that this morning has been something of a revelation to me.'

'Maybe if you met the others, they'd be a revelation too.'

She laughed. 'Okay, I admit, I'm busted. Promise me something though.' She turned and smiled at him. 'I don't *actually* want to meet them.'

He laughed too now, thinking how weird it would be if he did introduce Lorna to them. Even at the best of times they would have found it odd that he was friendly with someone who looked like that. Four days after the accident though, it would freak them out completely.

Perhaps it was because of that but he was really enjoying himself. He was just happy because she was easy-going and here they were inside this big old car like they were going on some kind of adventure. For once, he was almost looking after himself.

The final approach to the point was just a route marked out across the sands. He was mesmerized by the sound of the car on the soft surface, looking ahead to the small stone wharf with a couple of small white cottages, the dunes of the point stretching away, tall spiky grass growing across them in patchy clumps.

'What happens when the tide comes in?'

'It gets cut off.'

He liked the idea of being cut off there, unable to get back to campus and the real world.

'How do we know when the tide's coming in?'

'Don't worry, I always phone up and check the tides before coming out here.' She turned, more briefly than before, concentrating on the sand road, and said, 'I'm not just a scary face.'

'I think you have a very pretty face.'

She laughed. 'Thanks, I'll sleep easier now.' She drove up the stone ramp and parked on the wharf. There was smoke coming from the chimney on one of the cottages but there was no sign of anyone about.

They got out of the car and Will was immediately over-awed by the stillness, the clean feel of the air out there, the quiet. It was as if she'd spirited him away into another dimension. The town, the university, they weren't just a few miles away, they'd disappeared altogether, taking the rest of the world with them.

He looked down at the makeshift road they'd just come across, at the couple of small boats toppled over on their keels in the sand. There were some gulls floating about above them but even they were silent, like they could sense that nothing here was meant to shatter the peace.

He heard the boot shut and turned to see Lorna standing expectantly. Her face was so pale it was almost lost in the sunlight, and he wondered if he looked the same, two figures almost slipping out of reality, blurring like ghosts. Anything seemed possible in a place like this.

'What shall I carry?'

She looked at the things on the ground and said, 'If you don't mind carrying my bag and the sketch pad; that way, I can take pictures as we're walking.'

'Okay.' He picked up the small black doctor's bag and the sketch pad and followed her on to the narrow path that led away from the cottages and across the dunes.

She turned a couple of times as they were walking and took pictures of him and he smiled each time, not for the picture but because he couldn't help it. They reached the high point and she stopped, waiting for Will to come and stand with her.

The sea was far from the shore but blue and flat. The point stretched away to either side of them, the lighthouse far off to their left, the estuary behind them. And even now that he could see the geography of the place and knew where they were, it still felt like they'd been left behind by the world, lost in their own space.

She didn't say anything, just walked on further down the path into the dunes, closer to the beach. Finally she stopped and said, 'This looks good.' He stopped too and nodded agreement, looking around. 'You can put the things down.'

'Oh, right.' He put the things down, still unsure what to do next.

'This is it. Explore. Walk on the beach. Do whatever.' She held up her camera. 'I'll be taking pictures. Just give me a call if you need me.'

He nodded again and said, 'Thanks for bringing me.'

'You're welcome,' she said, still sounding like she couldn't quite work him out.

He walked down on to the beach and out on to the flats left by the receding tide. He headed for the sea but didn't get far before the sand beneath his feet was too waterlogged to feel safe. He was still far enough out that when he turned, the dunes of the point were reduced to a narrow strip of green. He couldn't see Lorna.

He faced out to sea. He liked being out there, feeling lost on the surface of the world, the blue sky vaulted, the sea running away to the gentle curve of the horizon. He liked the feeling of being reduced back to scale, in a place where it no longer mattered who he was, only a thin strip of green and a lighthouse to guide him home.

Walking back, he'd almost reached the beach when he saw Lorna, coming up over the top of one of the dunes. She pointed the camera at him and, he guessed, took a picture. She waited for him then.

'This is the most amazing place. How often do you come here?'

'I don't know. Every couple of weeks maybe. I was high out here once – that was pretty wild.' She looked around. 'It's probably better with a clear head though.'

He'd always assumed she was into drugs, the whole look of her.

'Marijuana?'

She smiled, because he'd called it marijuana which he supposed was a really square thing to call it.

'I don't smoke. Actually, it was acid.'

'Oh.' He'd never taken anything like that, had always been scared to, a fear that seemed ludicrous all of a sudden. In fact, if she'd had some with her he'd have probably taken it now, anything to help fix the memory of this day. 'Do you have any with you now?'

She laughed and said, 'Like you'd take it if I did!' He obviously looked stung or disappointed because she added, 'Look, as it happens I might have some mushrooms left in my bag, but you are clearly in one seriously strange mood today, or else you're just strange, and either way, you should think whether you really want to take something like that.'

'Magic mushrooms?'

She looked amazed and said, 'No, chanterelle mushrooms; I always like to keep some handy.'

'Let me take them.'

As if she hadn't heard him right she said, 'You want to take mushrooms?'

'Yes I do.'

She shrugged and walked away to where they'd left the bag and the sketch pad. He followed her and sat on the edge of the dune while she opened her doctor's bag and pulled out a plastic bag that had something dry and shredded in the bottom of it.

'There's less left than I thought. It should do you though.' She handed the bag to him and said, 'Just eat it.' He emptied some of the dry flakes into his hand and ate them, and as he chewed she said, 'It'll probably just play tricks with your vision, okay? You might hallucinate but not everyone does.'

He fought to swallow the first mouthful and said, 'I heard people think they can fly and jump off things.'

'Lucky there's no multi-storey car park out here.' He emptied the rest into his hand and took them. 'You want me to stay with you?' He shook his head. 'Okay, just wait for it to kick in or take a walk or something. I'm not going to be far away.' He smiled this time, because she sounded concerned and protective, and yet until this morning they'd probably never imagined speaking to each other.

She wandered off with her camera and he stayed sitting on the edge of the dune, looking out at the sea, his fingers playing absentmindedly in the cold sand. He wasn't sure how long he was sitting there before he noticed the changes. They crept up on him, his vision slowly expanding, the colours, the essence of things becoming stronger.

He picked up a handful of sand and watched it falling through his fingers, each grain radiating colour and light. Even his hand looked more real, possessed of an intricacy and beauty he'd never seen before. He looked up at the sky and was transfixed by its blue, a deep inviting blue he felt he could fall into and swim through.

He got up and started walking through the dunes. He liked this, the way he was still consciously him and yet his vision had been opened up. It was the same world he could see around him but with the dull surface torn away, exposing the reality beneath.

He'd been walking for a while when he heard someone call out. He turned and saw a child running between the dunes. There were other people out here. He followed and saw a glimpse again, not sure if it was a child now. Maybe it was Lorna or someone else. He walked on and as he cut between two of the dunes he saw the person ahead, sitting hunched on the sand, back towards him.

He moved forward slowly, trying to focus on the shape of the person sitting there. It kept changing in size, in colour, intensity, now a child, now someone bigger. He was only a few feet away when he heard a noise and stopped, distracted. It was something growling, like a large dog.

He looked at the back of the figure on the ground in front of him, hunched over, head bowed, face hidden. It was a child, he thought, and there was the growling again. He looked around, becoming fearful, back at the figure, and realized then, that the child itself was growling. If it was a child, whatever it was.

Will began to back away, disturbed now, and the growling was getting louder, more menacing, the shape threatening all of a sudden. He started to run and he could still hear it behind him and the dunes were confusing, the noise coming at him from different directions.

He heard his name called and stopped, the panic subsiding, his name again. He turned and Lorna was standing there. Morticia. It felt like hours since he'd seen her. She took hold of his face, looking into his eyes, and said, 'Just a little dilated!'

'There's a dog,' he said. 'It was chasing me.'

'There's no dog.' She took him by the arm and led him back to where their things were. 'Sit down here and relax.'

'There's a dog.'

'Don't worry, I'll protect you.' He believed her. He lay back in the sand and looked up at the blue of the sky again, finding it comforting and familiar. He couldn't hear the growling now anyway. All he could hear was the sea, a long way off, whispering gently.

He slept and when he woke it took a while to realize where he was and what he'd been doing. His vision was clear again. He felt like he'd slept a long time, as if the world had moved on while he'd been lying there. He lifted his head. Lorna was sitting on the side of the dune facing him, sketching, looking at him.

'How are you?'

'Good,' he said. 'How long have I been asleep?'

'Years,' she said and turned the sketch pad to show him. It was a picture of him sleeping.

'I like your drawing.' She smiled and looked at the picture herself. He thought of the experience with the mushrooms and said, 'That was amazing. I'm gonna do it again.'

She grimaced slightly and laughed, saying, 'Funny, I wouldn't have said it was your ideal drug of choice. Maybe you should stick to gin and tonic or sherry or something.'

Will laughed too, lying back in the sand. This was the best day he'd had in as long as he could remember. And she was real, true. She looked weird but she was completely genuine. He'd thought earlier how much it would freak the others out to be introduced to her but thinking of it now, he was certain Alex at least would appreciate how amazing she was.

He wouldn't tell them about her though, or about this day, certainly not about taking drugs. They'd look at him with even more thinly veiled unease if they thought he was spinning out of control on drugs, and they wouldn't understand anyway, certainly not Rob or Natalie.

He sat up and looked at Lorna. She'd still been working on the sketch but stopped now, surprised by his sudden movement.

'Thanks for looking after me.'

'That's okay.'

He wanted to say something else but didn't know how. He wanted to tell her that she was the truest person he'd ever met and he struggled with it for a while, finally thinking of something that he could say to her to show her that he was also true.

34

'Lorna, you know you mentioned that accident? The girl who was killed?'

She puzzled over his words and looked concerned then and said, 'Don't.' Her voice was urgent. 'Don't tell me.'

'I want to.'

She shook her head, troubled, saying eventually, 'No. Just tell me if you were driving.'

'No, I wasn't.'

She smiled warmly and said, 'Then that's all I need to know.' She put the sketch pad down. 'You should be careful, Will, particularly with people you've only just met.'

He nodded but he didn't feel like he had just met her. Some people could be trusted. He was one of them; the others maybe didn't think so, but he was. She was one of them too and he was glad she knew, glad that someone knew who would accept him for what he was, and not question him or wait for the cracks to show.

4

Matt bumped into Alex walking down the central spine. They nodded to each other and Matt said, 'Where you heading?'

'Psychology Department. You?'

'Library. You know how it is, that time in the term.'

'Yeah, I've got a shitload to do.' They were walking together towards the square now. 'Jesus, it's cold.' Matt shrugged and Alex said, 'What, you don't think so?'

'It's not New York cold.' He laughed, realizing how he'd sounded, and Alex laughed too. 'You sleeping any better?'

Alex shook his head but appeared unconcerned as he said, 'I don't think I've slept properly at all this last week.' He did look tired, but then the campus was full of tired-looking people at the moment, all trying to meet deadlines. And considering what lay behind his tiredness, Alex looked to be taking it all in his stride. 'What about you, Matt?'

'I'm the same, still wishing I'd done something afterwards.'

'You can't think like that. Don't think like that.' Alex looked at him, driving the message home. He sounded almost angry but softened and was more sympathetic as he said, 'It'll drive you insane if you think like that.'

'You're the psychologist,' said Matt and got a smile. 'I went for a drink with Rob last night. We were saying we didn't think it had been so bad. You know, there haven't been any police around the place. Most people seem to have forgotten it already.'

'Yeah, I think we'll be okay.' They'd reached the top of the steps in the square and stopped for a second, both aware that this was where their paths separated. 'How come you went for a drink and didn't ask me?'

Matt laughed, amused at Alex sounding left out, and said, 'We spoke to your better half; she said the two of you were watching a movie on TV.'

'Bitch,' said Alex, smiling too.

'We tried to ask Will as well but couldn't get hold of him.'

'Work,' said Alex by way of explanation. 'He was probably in the library.'

'Yeah, we figured. I might have a look for him in there now, just see how he is.'

'Okay, I might come and grab you for a coffee after this tutorial.'

'Sure. Later then.'

Alex headed straight down the steps and Matt cut diagonally across them, making for the library. He was left uneasy by the brief conversation with Alex, the first in days. They were all full of reassurances but there'd been a shift in the last week, as if they were all delicately trying to distance themselves from each other.

He'd mentioned going out for a drink with Rob but even that had been a cheerless couple of hours. The five of them had spent two and a half years living as a tight-knit clique, needing no one else, and now they couldn't think of anything to say to each other.

He couldn't help but think he was responsible for that too. If he'd stuck his ground and gone to the police they'd have had plenty to talk about, sympathy for his plight, vows to stick by him. In the light of this week though, he wasn't certain how much those vows would have been worth anyway.

He'd thought of the four of them, Alex and Rob especially, as the best friends he'd ever had and yet now there was a veneer of caution between them, like they'd all taken one step back towards being strangers. But then maybe that was the price to be paid for drinking, for driving too fast, for killing someone and leaving her in the road like she didn't matter.

He found a booth in the library, put his coat over the chair, his papers and bag on the table, then went in search of Will. He couldn't see him in the politics section, even checking the vacant booths to see if Will had left a coat the same way he had. He wasn't there though.

Matt was beginning to get concerned about Will. He'd hardly seen him about at all in the last few days, never answering his phone, never in the library. Alex clearly thought he was working hard but Matt wasn't so sure. Wherever Will was hanging out, Matt got the impression he was going to pieces over this, and that in turn made him think Will would be the one who got loose-tongued. And what kind of fix would he be in then?

He started to walk back to his own section but couldn't face it now, the thought of sitting in that enclosed booth with the silence oppressive around him and only historical journals to keep his mind from dwelling. Rob had done nothing but work for the past week and Matt couldn't see how he did it.

He headed downstairs to the small coffee bar and sat there in a corner where he couldn't be seen by people passing through the library lobby. He didn't want to be seen. None of the handful of people in the coffee bar were familiar but even in there, he wished he could be less visible, less big, like he could disappear into himself.

There were a couple of girls talking quietly at one of the clutter of tables in the middle of the room, all the other tables around theirs looking recently abandoned, cups still waiting to be cleared, ashtrays overflowing. It always looked like that though, the staff never too eager to tidy up.

Matt couldn't hear what the girls were saying because the couple on the next table along the wall from him were talking loudly and non-stop about the theatre. It was annoying him but he didn't say anything, just trying to shut it out instead while he watched the two girls.

They were both slight and pretty, both with long hair, one only marginally fairer than the other. Their faces looked alike too; anywhere but a university campus he'd have guessed at them being sisters. They had that aloof quality he often noticed in English girls.

He didn't know what it was but the English girls he found attractive always seemed so unapproachable, and when he spoke to them he always seemed to be saying the wrong thing, running up against brick walls. He still couldn't help looking though, being intrigued.

The theatre couple finally left. He still couldn't hear the girls at first but he looked down into his coffee and listened, picking up odd words, then more of the conversation. He heard the word 'funeral', his attention focusing more, realizing now that they were discussing something he knew about.

By the sound of it, the funeral had already taken place, something that seemed obvious when he thought about it and yet it hadn't occurred to him until now. One of them still sounded upset, the other offering words of comfort. He wanted to look up but felt like he'd be intruding if he did.

And then the comforter said she had to go and he heard the sound of her chair scraping the floor, her final words of assurance, footsteps. He looked up. The girl who'd left was the fairer one who'd been sitting in profile to him. The remaining one was almost facing him but her eyes were downcast.

Her friend was dead and she was upset, perhaps more so because the driver hadn't been found. That was a part of her grief he could ease even now by coming clean, but he wouldn't, as much for the others as himself. And maybe he really had left it too long now anyway.

She picked up her coffee cup and lifted it to her lips, and he noticed that her hand was shaking. She looked so small and vulnerable, lost in an untidy landscape of tables and chairs. He wanted to talk to her, offer her words of comfort, even if it made him a hypocrite to do so.

Her head sank a little and though it was barely perceptible he could see she was crying. He looked at the few other people in the room but none of them had noticed, and probably wouldn't have noticed if she'd been sobbing and wailing, another English trait he hadn't quite managed to get his head around.

He thought about it for a second or two. He could sit feeling sorry for himself, looking at this girl crying and knowing that indirectly it was his fault, or he could get up and go over to talk to her, ask if she was okay. She was one of those girls he didn't know how to handle but he couldn't sit there and watch her cry, because he couldn't sit by and watch anyone who needed help.

He got up and walked over, threading between a couple of tables. Typically, one of the other people in there looked up from his book as soon as Matt moved and watched his awkward progress towards the girl. She looked up only as he loomed over her, wiping her eyes, looking unfriendly all of a sudden.

Matt smiled and said, 'Are you okay?'

She pulled a slightly awkward face that made him feel like he'd tried to hit on her, unsuccessfully too.

'Please leave me alone.' Rebuffed. He never understood how or why, only that it happened. He thought of saying something, just to save face, but he couldn't see the point. He smiled as graciously as he could and turned to walk away. And then he heard her voice again, stronger. 'God, I'm sorry, that was really rude of me.'

He turned again and said, 'That's okay. I can understand you wanna be alone. I kind of wanna be alone myself.'

She smiled, her eyes red from where she'd rubbed them. 'So why did you come over?'

'Because you looked sad. You were crying.'

She nodded a little, as if she'd hoped nobody had noticed, and said, 'I don't really want to be alone.'

'Me either.' She gestured towards the seat her friend had been sitting in and he said, 'Can I get you another cup of coffee or something?'

'No, thanks.' He sat down, wondering how to proceed from there, conscious of the need to tread carefully. Before he could say anything though, she said, 'My friend was killed last week. You know that hit and run?'

'Yes I do. Emily Barratt.' She looked askance at him and by way of explanation he added, 'I didn't know her but I've heard a couple of people talking about her; she was in my college.'

'So we're in the same college too. You're not a JYA though?'

'No, fully paid-up member. I'm in my final year.' She nodded like it was something she'd been puzzling over for some time, showing an exaggerated interest. He found small talk painful anyway so he cut to the chase and said, 'What was she like? Your friend? If you don't mind me asking. It's just, you hear so many people talking about her like she's a statistic, it'd be nice to hear who she was.'

'Actually, what I hate is all the people who hardly knew her, who beat their breasts and say how sad they are and how close they were. It makes me sick. It's like they get a kick out of it.'

'That's true, people do that, like they wanna be a part of it.' He thought of Steve Herman, who'd died of some rare form of cancer in high school, the way the whole school had rallied around the memory of this kid hardly any of them had known, because he hadn't been that popular and hadn't been that nice. He didn't think it wise to share the memory, adding instead, 'You'd think people would wanna distance themselves from death, not associate themselves with it.'

She smiled, intrigued, and said, 'What's your name?'

'Matt MacAndrew.'

'Susie Hansen.' She reached out and shook his hand, laughing at how formal it seemed. Her hand was about half the size of his, a fragile feel to it.

'So what was she like?'

'Of course, sorry.' She sighed and said, 'It sounds so trite but she was a beautiful person, very kind, considerate. She'd be really quiet and then you'd get her talking about a book she liked, or a film or a place, anything, and she'd become really passionate, like nothing else mattered in the whole world.'

Matt nodded, though he couldn't get any real sense of her from Susie's description.

'Did she have a boyfriend?'

He guessed the question was pretty inconsiderate but Susie didn't appear to notice and said, 'She had a boyfriend from home but they split up at Christmas. I didn't like him much. She hadn't seen anyone since.' That thought appeared to trouble her. Her face froze, her eyes welling up again.

'What is it?'

She shook her head, unable to speak at first. Then she said, 'I just keep wondering what she was doing out there. We were at a party, in Broom Street.' His stomach coiled tightly at the mention of the street, the same party they'd been to.

'Maybe she was lost, just trying to head back into town.' Though now that he thought of it she was heading back in the other direction, he was certain of that, and now he was puzzled too and frustrated at not being able to share it.

'The thing is, she told me she was leaving and I just said "fine" and let her go. And we've never done that, but I didn't think she was walking home alone, I thought she was leaving with people.'

'You can't blame yourself.'

'I know, it's a terrible cliché but I can't help it.'

'But like you said, you thought she was okay. And even if you'd been with her, it doesn't mean she wouldn't have been knocked down. It was a party.'

'I know, you're right. I still can't help thinking it.' She looked towards the door, distracted for a second before she turned back and said, 'Matt – it was Matt, wasn't it?' He nodded, smiling. She looked like she was about to ask him some great favour but said simply, 'Do you want to go for a walk?'

'Sure. I'll just go and get my coat from the library.'

'Oh, look, don't bother. I've taken up enough of your time.'

'Nonsense. I wasn't in the mood for work anyway. That's why I was down here.' He stood and added, 'I'll be back in one minute.'

He went upstairs and picked up his coat, leaving his bag and books in the booth, convinced that if he had to go back for them he might do some work. As he headed back down the stairs he got the feeling she wouldn't be there, that she'd have changed her mind and left.

She was still sitting in the same place though and smiled as she saw him. She was really attractive, not just in the way she looked but her whole manner, and he was caught up in the anticipation of getting to know her, even while in the background he could hear a discordant note sounding.

He liked her but no good could come of this. If he got to know her it would be a friendship or relationship based on dishonesty and that lie would always be at the centre of things, a shadow. And the more the relationship came to mean, the more he'd be terrified of Will or one of the others getting careless.

He couldn't afford to confuse things like that. He'd go for a walk with her and that would have to be it. If she showed an interest in getting to know him better he'd have to play it busy, the build-up to finals and all that. For once he'd found a reason to talk to a girl he liked but he couldn't afford to forget what that reason was, that she was sad because he'd killed her friend.

They walked out across the square, past the chaplaincy centre and on to the paths that led down across the landscaped campus to the lake. It was cold but until he saw the green sweep of the campus frosted white he hadn't realized how cold. It was an amazing day, the first time in nearly three years that he'd seen the place looking like a true winter landscape.

'I love weather like this,' Susie said. 'It makes me think of Bruegel.' She looked at him apologetically and said, 'That wasn't meant to sound pretentious; it's just that I'm studying history of art.'

'No, it makes me think of Bruegel too. Or Hendrick Avercamp.' He laughed and said, 'What a great name! Hendrick Avercamp.'

She looked at him and said, 'You know a lot about art?'

He shook his head, saying, 'A great-aunt of mine owned a picture by Hendrick Avercamp, a winter landscape kind of like this. I used to stare at it for hours when I was a kid. I loved it.'

She looked entranced. 'You're serious? Your aunt owned an Avercamp?'

'Great-aunt,' he said.

'Was she rich?'

'Not at all.' He laughed at the thought. 'She married a really rich guy. They never had kids and then they divorced when she was like, forty-five or something. She said all she wanted was the house and the Avercamp. So he gave her those two things. She could have gotten a lot more but she didn't want anything. My grandfather had to make her an allowance because she had no money. When he died, my dad gave her an allowance. She was a great old girl but completely unworldly.'

'How wonderful.' She left a suitable pause and added, 'What happened to the painting?'

'She left it to a museum.'

'Oh.'

'Yeah, exactly. I dropped enough hints, but hey, she had this whole different drummer thing going. I'm happy anyway. It's sad to lock a great painting up in a private house.'

Susie looked up at him and smiled, saying, 'It's really weird but I already feel like I've known you for a long time.' He smiled too, feeling uncomfortable again though, because she was warming to him. He couldn't believe his bad timing. She seemed to realize then how much she was craning her neck and said, 'God, you're really tall.'

'You noticed?'

She laughed and said, 'Sorry, you must hear that all the

time.' She pointed off the path to a clump of trees, delicate and bare, drawn lightly in ink against the hazy white of the landscape.

They set off towards them, the grass crunching under their feet.

'This is a great spot. We had a picnic here last summer.'

'You and Emily?'

'And others. There were about six of us. It was such a lovely day.'

'Yeah, there have been one or two like that while I've been here.'

They stopped directly in front of the trees. Matt looked back at their two sets of footprints, dark dotted lines like animal trails. Susie swept the horizon with her hand and said, 'See what a great spot it is. The sea over there, the lake and the woods, the hills on the other side of the bay.'

He could tell she was going to cry and he was willing her not to. He'd have to comfort her if she did and he didn't want to build that bond any further. Again, he kept imagining how she'd look at him if it came out in a few weeks' time. He couldn't stand that, and would rather not get to know her at all than run the risk of it happening, having to see the accusation in her eyes.

Sure enough though, she started to cry, apologetically, trying to fight it, putting her hands up to cover her face. He put his arm around her and she cried into the front of his coat but didn't put her arms around him in return, a distance he was thankful for.

His own thoughts were going into freefall. As much as he liked this girl's company, as much as he was attracted to her, he wanted desperately to be away from her. He wanted to be away from everybody. Maybe that was it with Will too, that he simply found it easier to be alone because other people made him think more about it.

Yet Will hadn't even done anything wrong. That was why Matt should have gone to the police as soon as it had happened, to take the burden off the others and bring it into the open. He was the one who'd killed her, and maybe it hadn't been his fault but he'd turned himself into a guilty person by not owning up, guilty of something sordid and dishonest and cowardly.

Susie pulled away again, wiped her eyes, blew her nose.

'Sorry,' she said.

'Don't apologise. Jesus, your friend died; you'd have more reason to be sorry if you didn't cry.'

She nodded. 'It's stupid, I know, but I keep feeling guilty, because I let her leave that stupid party and because . . .' She stopped, fighting back another run of tears, swallowing hard like there was food stuck in her throat. When she spoke again she had to struggle to get the words out. 'It's because I didn't really appreciate what an amazing person she was, not until it was too late. I took it for granted, we all did. She was such a beautiful person and none of us noticed. Not enough.'

'I know,' he said. 'That's the trouble with great friendships. You often don't realize they were great until they're gone.'

She looked up at him, her eyes searching his as she said, 'Are you okay? You seem sad yourself.'

'I am a little sad today, but I'm okay.' He smiled as if to prove the point and said, 'Shall we walk back?'

They followed their own footsteps back to the path. As they walked up the hill again Matt glanced back, the lines of footprints making it look as though a handful of people had walked across to the trees, not just the two of them.

'So you're going back to the library now?'

'Yeah, I guess I should,' he said.

'Maybe I'll see you later then. We'll be in the bar tonight.'

She sounded hopeful and he couldn't resist asking, even though he was determined not to be there.

'Kirby Bar?' She nodded. 'Well, maybe I'll see you in there. I have like, a whole year's work to do but, hey, everyone needs a night off.'

She smiled and it made it easier to say bye, because she thought they'd be seeing each other again in a few hours. He went back up into the library and did one more sweep looking for Will before going back to his own booth. He'd been there twenty minutes or so before Alex came along and popped his head over the partition.

'Hey,' said Matt. 'I've only just sat down. I had a coffee downstairs, you know.'

'Sure.' Alex looked around. 'Is Will in here?' Matt shook his head and noticed the concern on Alex's face. He was glad he wasn't the only one worrying. 'Look, forget coffee. Come up later and we'll have a few drinks.'

'Sounds good,' said Matt. He thought of Susie and added, 'I don't wanna do a bar crawl though.'

'God, no, we'll just stay in Balmer.'

'Okay, I'll see you later then.' Someone nearby tutted and sighed loudly, irritated by the talking. Alex smiled and put his finger to his lips before walking away again.

He met them later, Rob and Alex and Natalie. Rob had finally managed to speak to Will on the phone and said he'd sounded fine except he was losing it over how much work he had left to do. Matt didn't believe it for a minute but it looked like the others did, because Will had always worked too hard.

The mood was better, almost the way it had been before. The unease was still there out on the edges of their conversation though. He noticed Natalie looking distant a couple of times, Rob more belligerent than usual, fired up, subtle differences. Alex was the only one who looked like he'd come to terms with it. Maybe that was just appearances but then Alex was that kind of guy, someone who dealt well with a crisis.

At one point Natalie said something about getting back to normal, the only time the accident was mentioned even indirectly. Alex looked confident and said, 'Don't worry, within a few weeks you won't even be asking that question. A few years from now you'll probably never think about it.'

Matt nodded in agreement, just to bolster Natalie, but he wasn't so sure. He thought of Susie, imagining her sitting now in Kirby Bar. He wondered if she was looking out for him, hoping he'd show. He liked to think so. The thought of her wouldn't shift then. He checked the clock behind the bar, just after nine, and, seizing the moment, he downed the remainder of his drink.

The other three looked at him and he said, 'I have to love you and leave you. I have work to do and parents to call.' They made a token effort at persuading him to stay for another drink but he was insistent and they gave in quickly. He wasn't sure if Rob looked suspicious but calling his parents was a pretty good excuse.

He walked out of Balmer and along the central spine to his own college. Kirby Bar was crowded, much busier. He walked in but made a point of not looking out for her; he wanted it to look almost like he'd forgotten she'd be in there. He went to the bar, got a drink and talked to a couple of guys he'd played rugby with in the first year.

He hadn't been there long though when someone tapped him on the arm. It was Susie. She'd obviously been home since earlier in the day because she'd changed and was wearing a thin sweater now with a cropped jacket over it. She smiled and said, 'Why don't you come over? We're sitting in that alcove over there.' He looked where she'd pointed, noticing the girl who'd been comforting her earlier in the day, a couple of other girls, two guys.

'Sure, I'll be over in a minute. Can I get you a drink?'

'No, thanks.' She went to walk away but said, 'Oh, I didn't want to say anything in front of the others, but thanks for earlier.'

'Don't mention it. I'll see you soon.'

She walked away and Matt took the banter from the rugby players. He stood with them for another five minutes or so, arguing in his head as to whether he should go over or not. It was bad enough drinking with Susie but the rest of them were probably friends of Emily Barratt too.

And yet wasn't that why he'd come down to Kirby in the first place? He'd come because he was attracted to Susie, and as much as it disturbed him, the connection with Emily Barratt made that attraction stronger somehow. There was something wrong in what he was doing but, even so, he downed his drink, got another and walked over to join them.

Susie introduced him. He noticed the other girl who'd been in the library looking at him quizzically, maybe wondering where she'd seen him before. The others were friendly though, asking him about America, what had made him come to England to study, all the usual questions.

He was sitting next to Susie and she spent quite a lot of time filling in the blanks of the conversation for him. They talked about more general stuff then, and increasingly the two of them were talking to each other rather than to the whole group. No one mentioned Emily Barratt.

When they rang time behind the bar, he said, 'You're welcome to come back to my room for coffee. Your friends too.' A discussion followed, the outcome falling the way he'd hoped, Susie agreeing but the others heading back into town. A couple of the girls, still feeling guilty maybe, wanted assurances that she'd be okay getting home on her own, and then it was done.

They walked back through the college to his room. He switched on the desk lamp, took his coat off, put the kettle on. Susie took her jacket off, then kicked her shoes off and sat up on the bed, cross-legged. He liked that she was comfortable there.

'Actually,' she said, 'I don't really feel like coffee. Do you have anything to drink?'

He switched the kettle off and looked around the room. He already knew the answer though, and said, 'Strange as it may sound, I have a bottle of Cointreau.'

She smiled and said, 'Perfect.' He felt pretty good, not drunk but that feeling of alcohol in his veins. He guessed she was a little drunk too. He poured a couple of drinks and then sat on the chair facing her.

They sipped at their drinks and sat in silence for a while and then she said, 'Why were you sad today? You said you were a little sad.'

'I'm not sure.' How could he even begin to tell her that he was sad because of the way things were with the others?

Emily Barratt had run in front of his car. He'd hit her and they'd left her there dead in the road, and in the process, somehow, their own friendship had been fatally injured too. It was unavoidably apparent whenever he saw them, that things weren't the same between them, would never be the same.

Alex had talked about things getting back to normal in a few weeks but Matt really wasn't so sure. And he thought maybe he'd been fooling himself, because he'd looked upon these people as the best friends he'd ever had, and yet for all their commitment to stick by him, he felt it was over, like he was on his own again, the friendship reduced to a shell.

He looked at Susie now and said, 'I think I'm sad because in a couple of months this'll all be over for me, and it's weird too, because partly I think I'm just homesick. I miss my little sister.'

She smiled and said, 'Tell me about her.'

He told her about Martha and then they talked about other things and had more Cointreau. He didn't even notice as the conversation slipped back to the subject that really connected them. Susie seemed to relish the chance to talk about it again and so he encouraged her, asking the right questions, listening intently.

She didn't say anything that gave him any more idea of who Emily Barratt had been. And as he listened he realized that what she was really doing here wasn't reminiscing on a dead friend, something she'd probably do with people who'd known her, but talking through her own guilt.

Maybe her friends didn't want to hear that but the pain was real, he could see it, could feel it himself. She looked on the verge of crying a couple of times, taking a sip of Cointreau on each occasion, calming herself. Finally though, she lowered her head and began to weep, her frame becoming even smaller, more vulnerable.

He put his glass down, went over and sat on the bed next to her, put a comforting hand tentatively on her shoulder. She responded immediately, holding on to him, crying into his shoulder, sobbing, the tears damp on his shirt. She was holding him tightly and he had his arms around her and he was embarrassed because it was turning him on.

After a while though, she pulled away slightly and looked at him, an intimate stare, seconds passing slowly. He dried her eyes with his fingers and kissed her, their mouths hot with the taste of alcohol and oranges. They kissed for a few minutes and then she began to unbutton his shirt but pulled away again briefly and said, 'I don't normally do this.'

'Me either,' he said, and he was telling the truth but he felt like a liar.

He was still confused by how they'd got to this stage and he was pretty certain she'd made all the running but she quickly became coy, asking if he could turn the light off when they were still only half undressed. And in bed she was timid, clinging to him but restrained, tense, so much so that he asked her a couple of times if she was okay.

She continued to cling on to him afterwards and eventually fell asleep like that. He wondered if that was all she'd wanted, the comfort of sleeping next to someone, taking the sex as part of the bargain. As he lay there on his back with her at his side he couldn't help but feel cheap somehow, used.

Yet she was the one who had the right to feel tricked. It was like a sick joke, sleeping with the friend of someone he'd killed, all the time pretending to comfort her. And the worst of it wasn't even that he'd killed Emily Barratt, but that he hadn't owned up, that he was able to walk through the rest of his time here like someone unblemished.

With the passing of every day he felt less like the kind of person he wanted to be, a person who believed in things that were right and decent, the kind of person he'd been brought up to be. And now there was this. For the sake of an easy and empty lay he'd made himself the lowest hypocrite.

He peered into the darkness above him. He hadn't slept with the light out since the accident, afraid of the dark – not in some supernatural way, a broader fear than that. It was as if he were losing himself, the person he'd been crumbling away like a structure fatally flawed.

It was worse in the dark because there was nothing to anchor him to the world, just the void, a void into which his whole being was dissipating. It was as if Susie would wake up in the morning and find nothing left of him. Maybe that would be the truth too, because the real Matt MacAndrew had ceased to exist before she'd even met him, and only the shed skin remained.

PART TWO

Ten Years Later

5

It was tempting, an easy suicide, to tip forward over the railing and be done with it, let nature take its course. It wasn't so much that he wanted to die, more that he'd run out of good reasons for living.

And the river was offering a way out, running high and fast. It was black and silent but the lights on the far bank caught the surface here and there and illuminated patches of swiftly moving water, taut and muscular and dangerous.

The water would be fiercely cold now, an instant numbing, perhaps enough for him to lose consciousness first. Even if he didn't, drowning was as good a way to go as any, swallowed up in darkness and dragged away into another night – no more thoughts, no more dreams, dispersed back into the void.

His body would be found at low tide perhaps, lying cold on the muddy bank further downstream, or maybe with the river flowing so fast he'd be carried out into the estuary or even out to sea. None of that would matter to him though, not any more – he'd be out of it.

And yet even as he thought about it and fantasized, he knew he wouldn't go through with it. That was who he was, someone who didn't have the nerve when it came to the moment of truth. It was so completely who he was, and he despised himself for it. He had nothing left to offer life but didn't have the guts to bow out gracefully.

He turned and leaned on the railing, looking up at the city's gothic outline and the clear black sky. It was cold and still at ground level but he could hear rogue gusts and squalls reverberating through the air high above him. A lone gull floated about in the dark, like a folded piece of paper caught on the wind.

It was probably nothing more than the sound of the wind but the atmosphere seemed charged somehow and he began to feel restless. He was trying to reason with himself but he felt a need to get back to the house, not for fear of being out but for fear of not being there when he needed to be.

That was ridiculous in itself, the feeling that he had any need to be in an empty house, a place where no one ever called, not in person, not even on the phone. He couldn't help but grasp on to it though, that sense of something portentous, and he began to walk now.

He crossed the road and up the steps, on to the steep path that led up behind the churchyard, kicking through the blanket of leaves that had been there for over a month. He skirted the castle walls then and down into the cobbled streets where the house was.

There was no one about. It was ten thirty but a Monday night, the town quiet. There were never many people around the old quarter at night anyway, no pubs or restaurants to draw people up there, hardly any of the buildings residential now.

As he walked he concentrated on the sound of his own steps, looking out for other people, not wanting to see anyone. He dreaded encountering other people at the best of times but especially tonight, the way his nerves were, the way he was almost expecting to be met by someone.

He heard something now and stopped. He turned, looking

about the street, his heart kicking a little with adrenaline, thumping awkwardly against his chest. The noise had come from a doorway where the shadows were piled up, a voice. He saw then that it was someone huddled in a sleeping bag, that he'd walked past without even noticing.

'Spare some change please?' That's what he'd heard, just a homeless girl, but it still unnerved him.

'Leave me alone,' he said and walked on, quicker, turning into the small close where his was the only inhabited building, surrounded by solicitors' offices, a stonemason's yard, a couple of buildings that had been sealed up for as long as he'd been there.

Stepping inside, he fell back against the door, on edge, mentally exhausted. He thought of the girl in the doorway and became angry with himself. Even if he hadn't wanted to give her money why had he spoken to her like that? And why didn't he want to give her money? She'd be better off with it than him.

He put his hand in his pocket and pulled out the notes he found there, a couple of twenties. He didn't have anything smaller and, again, he thought maybe it wasn't worth going back anyway. He put the money in his pocket and closed his eyes, trying to blank everything for a moment or two, but it was no good – the thought of that girl out there had set in like a virus.

He sprang off the door and out of it without even closing it behind him, almost running the fifty yards or so to where she'd been, worrying irrationally that she wouldn't be there. He slowed down as he approached the doorway, hoping she'd speak first.

She was silent though and he couldn't see her, just the edge of the grubby sleeping bag where it caught the stray edges of the streetlight.

'I'm sorry,' he said. 'I didn't mean to be rude. I just . . . Here, take this.' He put his hand in his pocket and took out the two twenties, offering them into the darkness. He didn't see the hand but felt it take the notes.

'Thanks, mister.' She sounded surprised though he guessed she didn't know how much it was. He stared into the doorway, thinking if he looked hard enough his eyes would adjust and he'd see her face. But maybe she didn't want to be seen and then he became nervous himself, an urgent sense that he really didn't want to see the face that was hidden away down there in the shadows.

'You're welcome,' he said and walked away quickly, looking behind a couple of times, embarrassed by how jittery he was tonight. He checked again when he got to his door that she wasn't behind him and having left it open for a few minutes he went through the place, checking that no one had come in.

It was another ten minutes or so before he was settling down, sitting at his desk upstairs with a whisky for comfort. He looked at his own pale reflection in the window, finally allowing himself to laugh a little at his own expense – it was crazy that he let himself get like this.

He needed to sell this place, move to another university, make a fresh start. For the four years that Kate had lived there the house had been okay, even if she'd always laughed and called it a body-snatcher's house. And he'd been okay too with her around, the attacks almost stopping completely.

But the two years since she'd gone had taken their toll, the house transforming into the place where he nurtured his demons, where he oversaw the crumbling of his own psyche. He was still holding it together during the day but he couldn't wait to get back any more, to sit here and dwell on the past and the moment it had all gone wrong.

One stupid moment, and it had become his whole life, his whole reason for being. He needed to make a fresh start and yet he worried that if he removed Emily Barratt from his life there'd be nothing left. He had less substance now than she did, less life in him.

He'd thought that many times over the last couple of years, that he inhabited this house like a ghost, no corporeal presence, no heat. It felt like a house that had been long left vacant, the absence of people cutting through the rooms like a draught. Maybe that was the problem, maybe the wrong person had died ten years before.

The glass was empty so he got up and crossed the room to where he'd left the bottle, pouring in another hefty measure before going back to the desk. He'd only just sat down again when a heavy knock sounded on the front door. It startled him and then left him paralysed.

People didn't knock on his door, not at that time of night, not ever. He didn't know what to do, panicked. Perhaps it was the girl. She might have seen him walk down that way and followed him, seeing the light on, the only house that was occupied. He thought of not answering but then remembered the way he'd felt down by the river, that there was a reason for him to come back.

He got up and went downstairs, put on the light, pulled the door open. There was no one there, just a plastic carrier bag on the step. It looked stuffed with papers, notebooks. He glanced down at it and leaned nervously out into the street, expecting again to see the girl walking away.

There was a guy standing a few yards away though, staring expectantly at the doorway. He'd given up and had been walking away but had heard the door. He too was some kind of traveller or homeless person, blond dreadlocks, a goatee, an old army backpack, a guy who looked like a smoked joint.

He nodded now and said, 'Oh, right.' He walked back a pace or two, stopping again as if a little unsure of getting too close. He pointed at the carrier bag and said, 'I just came to deliver that.'

'I think maybe you have the wrong place.'

The guy looked up at the house and took a piece of paper out of one of his coat pockets, studying it briefly.

'This is the right place,' he said. 'You're Dr Alex Stratton?'

'Yes, I am.'

'That's it. That bag's for you. I didn't know who else to give it to. His family didn't want it and I didn't know who else to give it to. I know he wrote to you sometimes.'

The guy had inched his way closer as he'd spoken but stopped short and almost took a step back as Alex said, 'Who? Who wrote to me?'

'Will. He died.' A name followed by two simple words of explanation, and yet Alex couldn't quite make sense of it, as if the part of his brain that was meant to process them had suffered some kind of short-circuit. He stared blankly at the guy in the street who looked vulnerable now, a young face beneath all that contrived earthiness. The guy looked upset, on the verge of breaking down, but instead he repeated himself like the words didn't make sense to him either. 'He died.'

Alex nodded and said, 'Please, come in. Have a drink or something.' He leaned down and picked up the carrier bag, taking it into the lounge without waiting to check that the guy had followed. He heard the front door shut though and the guy was standing there when he turned, looking around the room, slightly on edge.

'Sit down. Would you like a drink? Or coffee?'

'Just water please. Or caffeine-free tea if you have it.'

'I think I have fruit tea. The girl who lived here with me used to drink it. It's a couple of years old though.'

'That'd be cool. Fruit tea.' Alex nodded and went through into the kitchen.

Will was dead. It was a thought that sat awkwardly in his head. In a way he was shocked, just by the delivery of the news, but it wasn't a complete surprise. That's why he hadn't asked the obvious question, because he'd just assumed it had been the heroin Will had been addicted to for the last six or seven years.

The kettle was boiling so Alex walked back through into the lounge, intending to make small talk, act like the good host. The guy was sitting on the sofa though, hunched and con-templative over a small book that had the look of some kind of scripture about it.

He seemed oblivious so Alex went back out and finished making the tea, brewing one for himself too, blackberry and nettle, something he'd last drunk with Kate a couple of years before. He went back in then, hovering silently with the two mugs until the guy looked up and put the book back in his pocket.

'Sorry. Thanks. This is kind.'

Alex sat down in one of the armchairs and said, 'No, it's the least I could do after you brought this for me.'

He looked at the carrier bag where Alex had put it on the floor. 'It's his notebooks, letters, things like that. I thought you'd want them. I'm on my way up to a Buddhist retreat in Scotland so it's cool, you know, kind of on my way.'

Alex nodded and said, 'What's your name?'

'Luke.'

'And how did you know Will?'

Luke nodded thoughtfully, as though he'd been asked for his thoughts on some complex issue, saying finally, 'I met him a few years ago through a kind of mutual friend. I'd just graduated and he'd been kicked out of his squat so we were both looking for a place. That's it really, we became flatmates.'

'Was it an overdose?'

Luke looked uncomfortable but nodded, his expression suggesting he felt guilty or looked upon Will's death as a failure on his part. 'I was away for a couple of days. I found him when I got back.' He shook his head. 'It's crazy, you know, because he was really getting it together again, even talking about going back to college and stuff. He was developing a real interest in Taoism. That's why I wanted to get away after it happened. It was too weird, too scary.'

Alex couldn't quite work out what he was saying and was beginning to wonder why he'd invited this guy into his house. He was uncomfortable with the thought that he might have invited him in simply because he was lonely and wanted the company.

'Too scary in what way?'

'Will smoked it. He had a phobia of needles. I mean, like a real phobia.'

'I didn't know that.' He hadn't known either, that Will had smoked his heroin rather than injecting it. He hadn't known much at all about Will, and maybe he never had, even when they'd been friends, seeing him back then only as a caricature, the socially awkward stray they'd adopted, always relied upon to get drunk first, to be sick, to end up in scrapes. It wasn't the same person that Luke was talking about; this was someone real, with pain and emotions and hopes.

'I'm talking total phobia. And he had things under control again. So tell me, you know, tell me why he'd get stuff that was too pure, not from his regular guy, and stick it in his arm. That's what I told the police, search the place, you won't find another needle in here. Someone killed him. No way would Will have done that.'

'You're telling me Will was murdered.' Luke looked non-committal, not even meeting Alex's eyes. 'What did the police say?'

'They're looking into it.' He gave a knowing look and added, 'How hard will they look? That's the question. How hard will they look? How much do they care? You know, they have all this stuff to do and Will's just a junkie as far as they're concerned. Junkies OD.'

Alex tried to picture the kind of life they'd shared, Luke and Will. He wondered what their daily routine had been: meals, going out, the whole thing. Had there been girlfriends? It was hard to imagine too, which of them had been more dependent on the other. Whatever their domestic relationship, Luke was lost at sea now, unable even to comprehend how a junkie could die a junkie's death.

'Why would someone have killed him?'

'I don't know.' He looked despondent and Alex felt bad looking at him, realizing now that this guy had probably been a better friend to Will than he ever could have been.

They'd kept in touch by letter at first, more than he had with any of the others and Will had visited a couple of times, but the truth was Alex had slowly introduced distance between them. Whether or not it stemmed from the night of the accident, Will had begun to fall apart, Alex scared off by the risk of being tainted.

He stared at the bag, wondering for a moment or two if there were letters in there. His had become vaguely patronizing as far as he remembered, becoming less and less genuine. They'd stopped altogether just after Kate had left and yet Luke had brought these things to him.

Luke saw him looking at the bag and said, 'The police asked me if anything was missing. I told them there wasn't. Will didn't have much anyway, just the things in that bag. He'd even sold his books.' Alex looked up, not sure what to say, and noticed then that Luke was nervous, afraid even. 'I told them nothing was missing because I didn't think there was, but there is something missing.'

'Well, would you like to share with me what it is?' Alex's tone was sarcastic but Luke didn't appear to pick up on it.

'His scrapbook.' Luke didn't say any more, as if he were testing the water, and Alex was suspicious as a result. He'd seen Will's scrapbook a couple of times, full of newspaper cuttings of stories he'd found intriguing, almost half the book given over to the local press coverage of Emily Barratt's death and the fruitless search for the driver who'd killed her.

Alex shrugged now and said, 'Maybe he threw it away.'

'No.' Luke shook his head emphatically. 'He would never have thrown it away. And I saw it, the day before I went away, or two days before. It was taken.'

'What was in the scrapbook?'

'I don't know.' He was lying. 'All I know is someone killed Will, and the same person took it, but Will never told me anything about it. I don't know anything.'

Alex had been wondering whether this was going to turn into an opportunist attempt at blackmail. Luke was scared though, a fear that suggested he did know what was in the book, perhaps even that Will had told him about it. And now he was scared, the paranoia of someone who smoked too much dope.

Alex smiled sympathetically and said, 'This must've been

really upsetting. I know he was my friend too but I haven't had much contact with him in the last few years. I'm glad he was getting his life together again.'

Now that he'd said it he realized how inappropriate it sounded but Luke gave a little dignified nod like someone accepting condolences and said, 'He was a good person, one of the best people I ever knew. It just isn't fair, and I know life isn't fair but that doesn't make it any easier that this isn't fair.' Alex didn't say anything, not wanting to intrude on his grief. Luke paused too, as if looking for something positive to say. Finally he said, 'I dream about him, you know, nearly every night. I speak to him, and he knows he's dead. He's okay about it but at the end of each dream he says the same thing. He says, "You won't forget me, will you, Luke?" And I tell him not to worry, because I'll never forget him.'

Finally they were on to ground where Alex felt he could contribute something.

'You know, it's quite normal to dream conversations with the dead. Your mind has all this space set aside for someone who no longer exists. Dreaming offers a natural outlet.'

Luke smiled and said, 'It's what you do, isn't it? You study sleep? Sleep disturbances. Will told me a lot about it.'

'Yeah, it's what I do.'

'Well, it's kind of you to try and comfort me but I don't need it. He comes to me in my dreams.'

'Then maybe you should get him to tell you who killed him.' The words were out and Alex couldn't believe he'd said them, couldn't believe the lack of professionalism, the flip cruelty of it. 'God, I'm sorry, that was an appalling thing to say; I don't know what I was thinking.'

'It's okay, I understand. This must have been a shock for

67

you, too.' Even so, Luke finished his tea with a couple of long gulps now and added, 'I should go.'

Alex looked at his watch and said, 'Do you have somewhere to go? I mean, you're welcome to stay here if you'd like. The spare room's full of junk but you're welcome to crash on the sofa.' It seemed strange making an offer like that, as strange as if he'd invited the homeless girl back with him, but Luke looked uncomfortable anyway.

'No really, thanks and everything, but I'll be fine.' He looked swiftly around the room as though the thought of staying in that house unnerved him. 'Best that I make a move.'

He stood up but Alex stood with him and said, 'What is it? You can tell me. Something about this house?'

He smiled apologetically and said, 'You're a scientist but I'm not, you know. You're okay with this place, I can see that, and it's cool. I just know I couldn't stay here. There's a vibe, that's all.'

Alex produced a knee-jerk laugh and said, 'If there are any bad vibes in this place they're probably coming off me.'

'No,' said Luke, earnest and insistent, putting his hand out to shake Alex's. 'No, you're good, and thanks for your kindness. I meant no disrespect.'

'You didn't show any.'

Luke looked around again, as if confirming his suspicions about the house and its bad vibe, whatever it was. When his gaze came back to Alex he said, 'I hope we'll meet again some time.' It was a new age sentiment, something he probably said to everyone he met.

'Sure,' said Alex and walked out to the door with him.

They shook hands again, Luke clasping Alex's hand in both of his own before walking away. He stopped and turned after a few yards though, almost in the spot where Alex had first seen him. He looked lost in thought for a second before saying finally, 'Will was murdered. It's important that you believe me. It's important I'm not the only one who knows the truth.'

'I believe you,' said Alex, empty words, meaning nothing. And satisfied, Luke walked away up the street.

Alex stared after him until he'd disappeared, wondering where he would go at that time of night, how his onward journey to Scotland would unfold. He envied him somehow, envied him his certainties, and the comfort with which he was willing to set off into the empty night rather than stay in his house. Maybe he just envied him for not being Alex Stratton.

Back inside he picked up the carrier bag and took it upstairs to his study. He downed the whisky and poured another and sat back at the desk, emptying the carrier bag item by item. There were notebooks filled with amateurish sketches, rambling verses of poetry, drugged-up philosophy.

There were some letters but none from him or from anyone whose name he recognized. The only thing of interest was the item that was missing, the scrapbook. And perhaps that wasn't worthy of too much consideration, Luke hardly striking him as the most reliable witness.

He still couldn't help but turn over the implications, trying to calculate the chances that it had something to do with them, with the accident. If Will had been murdered and the scrapbook had been taken by the killer . . . His thoughts seized, unable to get past words like 'murdered' and 'killer'. It was absurd.

He picked up the glass of whisky and took a sip, savouring the taste, concentrating on it, trying to put away everything else. He was still on edge, twitching with every stray sound around the house. It was nothing to do with Luke's visit, this a part of the edginess that was his regular companion.

Finally he heard something from downstairs that got him out of his chair, heart thumping. It sounded like something being moved, or a cupboard door being closed, enough to convince him that someone might be down there, that perhaps he hadn't closed the front door properly.

He crept down the stairs, checked the door, moved slowly through the downstairs rooms, a self-induced chill dancing up his spine. There was no one down there but his nerves were doing party tricks, a constant sense that he was about to hear something else, or catch some movement at the edges of his vision.

It was him of course, not something in the house itself. He'd been spooked down by the river, then by the girl in the doorway, by her voice, the talk of Will's death probably not helping either. All these little coincidences that meant nothing had stacked up on top of each other, his rationality unravelling around them.

He turned off the downstairs lights and went up to the bathroom to get ready for bed. A part of him was tempted to put it off, knowing what would happen when sleep came, but in the end it was better to face up to it and make use of it. Anyway, sometimes when he tried to put it off it made things worse.

He'd have an attack tonight whatever he did. He'd been thinking of her again all day, and then with the evening's developments on top, he could almost guarantee it. But it was all in his own mind, that was the thing to remember, that none of it was external, none of it was real.

He set up the equipment once he was in the bedroom, turning on the video recorders, checking that he hadn't accidentally moved them off target, one covering the bed, one covering the door. He strapped the actimeter to his wrist then and turned out the light.

He was tired but couldn't help feeling the familiar knotting-up of dread, knowing what lay ahead of him. He touched the wrist monitor with his other hand, as if reminding himself that this was just a scientific experiment, and concentrated on his breathing, letting his thoughts fall away.

He knew what lay ahead in the darkness, not the specifics but the generalized terror and fear of it. He knew, and yet he lay there on his back surrendering to it because it was who he'd become, the victim of his own mind, his own history.

She'd torment him again tonight, just like she had for the last ten years, and it was right that she do so, something only the two of them would ever understand. It was their history and it had to be relived.

6

This was Will's life, spread out before him on his desk. It didn't add up to much but it made Alex question what kind of people his family were that they hadn't wanted it. He had some vague recollection that they hadn't been supportive people, not even back at college. It left him wondering how they'd have responded to Luke's claims that Will had been murdered.

Alex had been doubtful but surely any normal family would have clung on to that, out of a desire for justice or truth, or for the minimal comfort of knowing their son's heroin overdose hadn't been self-inflicted. Any normal family would have scoured these possessions the way he had for the last hour, searching for even the slightest link to a possible murderer or motive.

He'd found nothing though, and, having met Luke even briefly, he could imagine him not telling Will's family about his suspicions anyway, out of respect for their grief or just because he'd have seen it for the futile gesture it was. No one else cared about how Will had died, no one else except, perhaps, Dr Alex Stratton.

He leaned back in his chair and looked around the office, the picture of his parents with him in his doctoral gowns, a picture of his brother Julian in the same get-up, a real doctor, someone who made people better and yet still found time to read every article and book Alex wrote.

Two of the prints were from Julian too, the Escher and the Geiger, both of them fitting for someone who studied the demons of troubled sleep. On the wall facing him was a picture Kate had given him, a Glen Baxter print, because he'd needed to lighten up – that's what she'd told him. And then there was his film poster, framed now, the only thing that had survived from his old student rooms.

It was a good place to be, this office, a positive place, somewhere that reminded him of what he had to be thankful for. On a superficial level at least, he'd thrived over the last ten years, and there were people who cared about him, and he'd had more than was perhaps his fair share of happiness.

He felt optimistic now as he looked around, and he was glad he'd come in. He was officially on sabbatical and he'd thought about staying home but had come in as usual to be around for Ruth, in case she needed him for anything. It was better anyway that he'd been there looking through Will's things rather than back at the house.

Collecting them up, he began to put them back in the bag. He'd keep them but there wasn't anything there of the Will he remembered, nothing either that would add anything to his death. And yet even as he dismissed it, he couldn't shake off the thought of the missing scrapbook.

It would keep nagging at him, he knew it, and it meant nothing, only that Will had tried to free his mind of her by finally throwing it away, or that Luke had simply been unable to find it. Luke had been scared though, and Alex couldn't help but give space to the quietly disturbing possibility that he'd been right to be afraid.

Without thinking about it he picked up the phone, dialled directory enquiries and asked for the number for the Brighton police. He just wanted to be told by someone official that there had been nothing suspicious about Will's death, that Luke had been blinded by his own loyalty and friendship, that their friend had died a junkie's death.

When he got through he asked to speak to someone about the death of William Shaw but ended up just giving his own details, offered a promise that someone would call him back as soon as they were available. He put the phone down, frustrated.

A knock sounded on the door. It was Ruth.

'Come in.' She walked in smiling, looking tired. She was small anyway and wore her hair short, and when she was tired she looked like a little kid, like she was too young to be a student, let alone researching a doctorate. 'Ruth, I've been telling you for two years now that you don't need to knock.'

'I just think it's good to let you know I'm coming. You never know, it might be inappropriate for me to come in.'

He smiled too and got up to make coffee, saying, 'It's a sad indictment of my life perhaps, but trust me, it's always appropriate.' She sat down, laughing now, and he said, 'Anyway, you're looking pretty wrecked this morning – take it you've been in the lab all night?'

'Yeah, I had two volunteers in.'

'Anything interesting?'

'Not really. I think one of them just wanted a quiet night's sleep.' Alex smiled. 'But I'm not the only one looking wrecked this morning. Care to talk about it?'

'Nothing to talk about,' he said, continuing with the coffee, trying to dismiss it. 'Yeah, I had an episode but it was nothing out of the ordinary.'

'Alex?'

'Ruth?' He said, mimicking her accusatory tone.

She backed down, probably just too tired, and said, 'Okay,

but I'm willing to state yet again for the record that I'd like *you* to go in the lab for me, and that if you really cared about my doctorate you'd volunteer happily.' She laughed, an admission perhaps of how outrageous it was to suggest he didn't care about her research.

He laughed it off too but couldn't resist saying, 'Let me remind *you* yet again of the advice I gave you when you first approached me with a doctorate in mind.'

'I know,' she said, reciting it like something she'd learned by rote, 'go to the University of Florida, study under Douglas and Dambrauskas.'

'You can't deny they're where the heat is in sleep research at the moment.'

'Generalized sleep research, yes. But ours is a specialized interest, isn't it, Dr Stratton? And with a PhD supervised by you, I'd say Douglas and Dambrauskas would look upon me as an equal, not as a potential student.'

'The ugly face of raw ambition.' He was about to continue but the phone rang. He picked it up. 'Dr Stratton.'

'Dr Stratton, it's DC Holder, Sussex Police. You called us about the death of William Shaw.'

'Yes, yes I did.' Ruth looked at him and gestured, asking if he wanted her to leave. He shook his head and said into the phone, 'I'm sorry for troubling you but I'm an old college friend of Will's and I've only just found out. I wanted to know what had happened, get things straight.'

There was a sigh at the other end, the guy unhappy perhaps that this one was a time-waster. 'I see. Your friend was a known drug user, Dr Stratton. Initially, the death was treated as suspicious, primarily because of information given to us by Mr Shaw's flatmate.'

'About the needle?'

75

'So you've spoken to Mr Boniface?'

'Yes,' said Alex, guessing that he was talking about Luke. 'It's true though, Will would never have used a needle.'

He wanted to hear how the policeman would respond to that but there was just another sigh and a tired voice saying, 'As I said, Dr Stratton, we did treat the death as suspicious at first but we haven't been able to find any evidence to suggest that Mr Shaw was murdered, no sign of any force involved in administering the drug, no sign of a forced entry to the house. All I can say is that a phobia doesn't count for much when you put it up against the craving an addict experiences for heroin.'

'I suppose you're right.' He felt reassured and yet the guy hadn't really told him very much. 'So there were no indications at all that he might have been murdered, no motives, no enemies?' He was conscious of Ruth, trying not to listen but looking shocked by what he'd just said. At the other end of the phone there was a pause. Alex could hear other people now in the background, other phones ringing, the sense of a busy office, real investigations that he was hampering.

'We've explored all the possible angles you've mentioned and I'm afraid it's looking increasingly likely that your friend's death is exactly what it appears to be, a self-administered overdose. Unless, of course, you have some information that might suggest otherwise; we're always willing to explore a new lead.' He was being sarcastic but Alex felt uncomfortable, conscious that the only extra information he had related to a completely different death, one that had also never been properly explained.

'No, I'm sorry if I've wasted your time. I just wanted to be certain.'

DC Holder had sounded irritated throughout the call but seemed to soften now, possibly seeing through the annoyance of dealing with a time-waster to someone who'd lost a friend, who maybe felt guilty that he hadn't done more.

'Not at all. I'm sorry about your friend.'

'Thank you.'

'And, Dr Stratton, if anything else does come to light, we'll look into it. Don't think we don't take Mr Shaw's death seriously.'

'That's good to know. Thanks.' He put the phone down and said by way of explanation to Ruth, 'An old friend of mine died of an overdose. I found out last night.'

'Oh, I'm sorry.' She looked a little awkward, saying after a moment or two, 'Was there some doubt about it being an overdose?'

Alex looked dismissive and said, 'No. No, not at all. It was just his flatmate, the guy who told me. He's a real flake, mystical religious type. Anyway, he was convinced that Will had been killed.'

'His name was Will?' She looked sad, an appearance exaggerated by her sleepless eyes, glazed and struggling. Alex envied her, who she was, her feelings, the freedom she still had ahead of her. Every now and then he wanted to tell her urgently to get out of there, go to the University of Florida. That was how he felt now, not wanting her to show an interest in what had happened to his life. Instead though, he simply answered her question.

'Yeah, his name was Will. He was a politics student in my year. Went off the rails a bit after graduation, been a heroin addict for the last six or seven years. Still a bit of a shock though.' He thought briefly of the previous night, not of when Luke had given him the news but of the hours afterwards, sleep.

As if reading his thoughts, she said, 'So did that play any part in what happened last night?'

He knew that she was asking about the attack; it even gave him a certain amount of pleasure that she was so driven by professional curiosity. 'Not directly. I'm assuming it must have been a factor but I have no recollection of Will featuring in my dreams.'

'No sense of him being present in the room?' Alex shook his head. 'But the other person was present?'

'Yeah, she was present.'

Ruth looked frustrated, a point she always reached in their conversations about Alex's sleep problems. She didn't say anything because she didn't need to repeat it, that if he'd allow her to study him they might find out who this person was, maybe even get to the bottom of it, bring the attacks to an end.

She'd made her case on countless occasions and, as far as Alex could tell, she'd never once considered the fact he might be lying, never contemplated the possibility that he knew all too well the identity of the person at the centre of these disturbances. He knew who she was, and he knew there was no cure Ruth could offer that would remove her.

By way of consolation now, he said, 'There was something interesting last night, apart from the attack – some automatic behaviour.'

She looked intrigued, leaning forward in her chair as she said, 'Sleepwalking?' He nodded. 'Did you get it on video?' He nodded again, smiling as he got up because he'd already decided to let her see it, had even left the video lined up.

'I used to sleepwalk as a child, not very often but enough. As far as I know, this is the first time since.'

She got up and came over, standing just behind him as he switched on the television and video and pressed play. He took a step back then so that they were standing next to each other, watching Alex in bed in the ghostly light of the infrared, not moving at first, the outline of his body only just visible.

He sat up as if pulled by strings, and, watching himself for the third time that morning, Alex felt his spine chill. The first time had been the worst, fast-forwarding through the tape earlier; the sudden speeded-up movement had startled him and left him shaking. Even with familiarity it was still uncomfortable viewing.

The sleeping Alex on the screen looked like someone in a trance, but he also had the unmistakable look of someone being called, summoned to another part of the house by an unheard voice. He got out of the bed and walked out of camera shot, Alex hitting the fast forward button, an unchanging image of the empty bed flickering before them.

Ruth said, 'How long?'

'Seventeen minutes.'

'Wow.' She stood in silence watching. A sudden movement appeared on screen as Alex reappeared, comically fast as he got back into bed. He wound it back and replayed it at normal speed. He looked completely unruffled, still in a trance, no change in his appearance.

He took the video out now and put the other in, the one that focused on the door of the bedroom. Again, initially it showed just the empty door frame but then Alex emerged into the shot and walked through the door. He stopped it and rewound a little.

'Look what happens just after I walk through the door.' They watched again.

The sleeping Alex repeated his steps towards the door and stopped for a moment on the other side of it and looked over the balustrade to his right, down the stairs, as if making certain where he was being called from. He moved on then, out of shot across the landing before reappearing in the shadows as he disappeared down the stairs.

He hit fast forward, stopping short this time, thirty seconds of eerily empty infrared before he appeared again walking up the stairs, out of shot, then back towards the camera, not hesitating now as he made his way past and towards the bed. Alex stepped forward and turned it off, and sat on the edge of his desk as Ruth sat back in her chair.

'It's a long shot but I take it you have no recollection?'

'No, but I was on edge earlier in the evening, kept thinking I could hear noises downstairs. Maybe that was it.'

She nodded but shuddered a little as she thought about it, and said, 'Very unscientific, I know, but doesn't it give you the creeps watching it?'

'No. And you're right, that's not very scientific.' He was lying of course, or lying in part. It gave him the creeps, but he was determined to dispel that feeling with his knowledge of the science that lay behind what they'd seen in the video. It was automatic behaviour, sleepwalking, an unusual and interesting phenomenon but one that was no more mysterious than migraine or any number of other conditions.

Chastened, Ruth said, 'Had you moved anything downstairs, as far as you could tell?'

He shook his head and they sat in silence for a while, Alex certain that both of them were wondering exactly what he'd been doing during those seventeen minutes.

The curiosity was twofold: partly a desire for more cameras, more physical evidence, but a gnawing need to know, too, what subconscious world it was he'd walked through, who he'd seen there and who had called him, if anyone.

The person in the video was almost as much a stranger to Alex as he was to Ruth, and Alex had no idea what had been going on in the depths of his mind as he'd walked through the house in sleep. It could have been triggered by something completely innocuous. At the same time though, he couldn't help but think of the voices that might have called out to him in the night.

Finally, he said, 'Well, as I didn't have cameras downstairs I suppose we'll just have to speculate.'

'I suppose so. Though of course, I'm still not sure why you use the cameras at all.' He smiled, because she was teasing him, making clear that she knew his sleep disturbances were more than he liked her to believe.

He was about to dismiss what she'd said but for once decided at least to open up a little, nodding as he said, 'I try always to be scientific, you know that, but when unpleasant things happen in your sleep . . .' He trailed off before saying, 'I just like to look at these tapes, to reinforce what I already know, that these attacks are internal, products of my own mind and nothing else. It's stupid, I know, but it makes me feel better.'

She looked surprised, even touched, by the sudden admission of fallibility, and said, 'It isn't stupid at all.' She smiled then.

'What?'

'Nothing,' she said, making no attempt to sound convincing. 'Just nice to see a chink in the emotional armour. Maybe I'll break down your defences yet, find out your secrets.'

He responded with an easy laugh and said, 'I have no idea what you're talking about.' He was almost telling the truth too, because he still didn't see himself as a secretive person.

He had an image of himself as someone who was open, and yet in truth he'd become secretive by default, never wanting to talk about anything that might lead back into the past. It was the way he had to be, always wary of unearthing the one secret that had spread its roots into every part of his life.

And it wasn't even as if he was defending himself with this secrecy. He'd stopped caring a long time ago about the consequences on his own life of going to the police. Going to the police: it seemed laughable now after all this time, and anyway, what did he have to lose? There was nothing they could take from him that he hadn't already shed.

But it had been a group decision, and so he'd kept it secret for them, never telling anyone. He'd kept it secret to protect four friends, and now one of those friends was dead, and Alex was beginning to wonder if he should let the remaining three know about it, and the circumstances involved.

A phobia of needles, a missing scrapbook; even given the value Luke had attached to them, these things hardly added up to a suspicious death. Luke was paranoid, and for a while it had looked like rubbing off on Alex but, like the policeman had said, Will's death was probably exactly what it appeared to be.

He'd still tell the others though, even about what Luke had said, giving them the chance to draw their own conclusions. Possibly, too, they'd simply want to know that someone who'd once been a close friend of theirs had died in a Brighton flat with too much heroin in his blood, his life unmarked, a person almost unloved.

And the thought of Will being unloved made him feel guilty too, because he wasn't really doing it for Will but for himself, the death providing him with a reason to get in touch again. He hadn't spoken to any of them since graduation and it felt now as if by making contact he could turn the clock back and undo the gradual descent of the last ten years.

It was like a chance to go back to a better time and, impossible as he knew it was, a chance somehow to make things right. He could never put right the simple and devastating wrongs of that night and the days afterwards but perhaps Will's death was finally offering him a chance to come to terms with it, and perhaps even to forgive himself.

7

He was back home early in the afternoon. He took the bag of Will's things up to the spare room and found a spot there for it amongst the accumulated junk. A lot of it was stuff Kate had left, kept there as part of the charade they still played, that she'd come back, that Columbia was just a temporary thing.

They'd been happy together. Early on he thought maybe they'd even loved each other, but in the end they'd just been happy and that hadn't been enough, not to counter the promise of Kate's career, nor his own morbid determination to stay exactly where he was.

In the first twelve months her e-mails had been full of suggestions that he follow her out there, and the one trip he'd made to see her had ended up like a glossy sales pitch. Then she'd given up, and though she'd never said anything he got the feeling she was probably seeing someone else now. He hoped so anyway.

He closed the door behind him and made to walk to the study but hesitated, looking at the stairs, snagged by the memory of the video. He walked down a flight and retraced his filmed steps from the bedroom door, down the second flight to the ground floor, hesitating again in the hallway.

The kitchen seemed the most obvious place he'd have walked in his sleep but standing there he felt drawn to the lounge instead. He followed his instincts and walked through, staring around the room again for any sign that he'd been in there during the night. Seeing nothing obvious, he edged around the room, studying everything in more detail, studying the bookshelves in particular, finding nothing.

Finally he walked through into the kitchen. He'd been in there briefly that morning and had looked around. He'd seen nothing and was surprised now that he hadn't noticed the book on the table, an old paperback collection of East European poetry, picked at random no doubt from the shelves in the lounge.

He sat down and flicked through its pages. He assumed this is what he'd done for the lost seventeen minutes the previous night. He'd gone into the lounge, taken a book off the shelf, brought it into the kitchen and sat at the table with it as if reading.

Looking at it now made him wistful, partly because of the mournful poems, Mandelstam, Akhmatova, Milosz, partly because it was a book from his pre-university days. The person who'd first read these poems had been a romantic, learning them, reading them aloud. It was a wonder where he'd gone.

He'd grown up, he supposed, moved on. He took the book with him now, up to the study. He'd show it to Ruth tomorrow, fill in the blanks, let her keep it if she was interested. And as his rational mind had known all along, there'd been a mundane reality behind what had happened last night, behind the sleepwalking at least.

Once in the study he opened the drawer in the desk where he kept his address books and diaries. He had nothing for Natalie or Matt, only their parents' addresses. He had a contact for Rob though. The two of them had exchanged Christmas cards every year, always updating addresses, saying how they should get together some time.

About seven years ago Rob had left a message on Alex's answering machine but that was as close as they'd ever come to real contact. And now, finally, he was about to return the call, even though Rob probably wouldn't be there, somewhere in central Africa instead, reporting on some grisly conflict for the *Telegraph*.

He rang the number, listened to Rob's voice on the answer-message, unchanged and oddly familiar after all this time, waited for the beep.

'Hi, Rob, it's Alex, er . . . Alex Stratton. I'm guessing you're overseas but if—'

He was cut short by a click at the other end and Rob's voice saying, 'No, Alex, I'm here. I was screening.' Alex was thrown, and after a moment's silence Rob added, 'Amazing. Amazing. Jesus, it's good to hear from you.'

'I thought you'd be in Africa,' said Alex, aware of how lame he sounded but still stunned that Rob had answered.

'No, I'm finished out there. Got a gig in Kosovo. That's why I was screening: I'm leaving in a couple of days and there's a shitload to do.'

'Kosovo?'

'Yeah, not as odd as it sounds. I was in Bosnia for Reuters before I ever went to Africa so I'm an old Balkan hand. Anyway, forget that! I mean, this is momentous. Alex Stratton finally graces me with a phone call.'

'I know,' said Alex. 'I've been meaning to get in touch for years but you know how it is. Have you kept in touch with the others?'

'Only Nat really, phone call every year or so. Had a couple of letters from Will but that dropped off pretty quickly. And Matt, Matt just slipped off the radar from the minute we left. Have you heard anything from him?'

'No. Listen, Rob, the reason I'm calling, I found out last night, Will died of a drug overdose.' There was silence at the other end, enough that eventually he added, 'Are you still there?'

'Yeah, I'm still here.' There was another pause before Rob spoke again, his tone one of somebody who simply didn't know how to react, who perhaps thought he should be saddened and yet wasn't. 'I don't know what to say. I mean, Jesus, it's terrible. I haven't seen him in ten years though. It wasn't intentional, was it?'

He didn't need to know, was just asking what seemed like the right question, but all the same, Alex said, 'They don't think so. He'd been an addict for six or seven years: heroin. Truth is, Rob, he never got over the accident.'

Alex could sense the sudden discomfort at the other end of the line, as if Rob were uneasy that it had been brought up, or maybe that Alex was discussing it over the phone. When he spoke again his voice was reined in, the words carefully chosen.

'The same could be said of anyone involved in a situation like that. Some people deal with it better than others I suppose.' He stopped, hesitated, and then more relaxed said, 'Listen, Alex, why don't you come down for lunch tomorrow? Or I'll come to you if you're busy. I really do have a shitload to do but wouldn't it be great, I mean, to see each other, catch up properly?'

Alex thought about it. His instinct was to say no, that he couldn't, that it was too far, but he wanted to talk openly to Rob now, to get another opinion on Will's death from within the dormant circle of their friendship. It was already clear that Rob was uncomfortable talking about it on the phone so Alex agreed, checking on the address, giving an estimate of the time he'd arrive.

It was only after he'd put the phone down that he wondered why Rob had been so cagey. He supposed a certain amount of caution was understandable from someone who'd been a journalist in the kind of countries where phones were tapped, where there was always some kind of war footing.

He still couldn't understand why Rob would apply that same caution to the accident in their own past though. They'd agreed to keep it secret and Alex had played along with that, would continue to play along, but it wasn't something bad enough to fear talking about it with each other on the phone.

Possibly Rob was just mixing up the things they'd all mixed up so badly when it had happened, the way it felt to them and the way it was in the real world. They'd been devastated by the turn of events that night, not in an obvious way, but with a subsidence that had gradually undermined who they were, forcing them apart, isolating them from each other.

If they'd gone to the police on the night it had happened Matt would have been hung out to dry for the couple of drinks he'd had, but beyond that, in the real world, they'd been victims too. She'd run in front of their car, her death as random and unavoidable an act as if a rabbit had sprinted beneath their wheels.

Yet something about the argument in his own head rung false. His own subconscious was telling him every night that he was no victim of circumstance. It wasn't Emily Barratt who inhabited the dark edges of his sleep, it was his own knowledge of her death. He wasn't being haunted by her but by himself, by the person he'd been that night ten years before.

It played on his mind for the rest of the afternoon. He tried to work but, as so often happened lately, he shuffled his notes and spent most of the time staring out at the fading light beyond the window. He'd have no peace tonight; he could sense it already.

The uneasiness started when he was making dinner, the sensation of someone crossing the hallway just outside his vision, like a stirring of air, as if somebody had crossed swiftly from the lounge to the stairs. He dismissed it but kept picking up the stray sounds of the floorboards above him, the house coming alive.

He sat at the kitchen table to eat and had stopped hearing the noises above when he noticed he was shivering. He told himself it was a cold room anyway, that with the stoves off the temperature would have dropped naturally. He couldn't shake it off though, the nagging sense that there was a presence of some kind in the house with him.

That was how it went on throughout the evening, sitting in his study, trying to ignore the constant feeling that someone else was in the house, moving about just beyond the scope of his hearing and vision, teasing him, laying siege to his psyche.

Before bed, he performed another of his routines, systematically checking the rooms, the doors, the windows, reinforcing what he always knew, that he was alone. And then he set up the equipment, a reminder of his other constant defence, that the explanation for his unease lay within the world of science.

Once in bed, he knew it was too late to try and govern what would come in the next few hours. He could only lie there and try to relax. He even reminded himself of another remote possibility, that an attack might not come tonight after all. But he wasn't hopeful, trying instead to prepare himself for what might come.

It was a mild night but full with a volatile breeze that toyed with the curtains and tested the house here and there. There was no noise inside in the darkness of his bedroom, just the sensed noise of the electrical equipment that surrounded him and the intrusive mumbling of his own thoughts.

He touched the actimeter and thought himself through the process that lay ahead, reassuring himself that it was a physiological process that he knew and understood. Maybe he wouldn't have an attack tonight anyway, not after the severity of the one the night before.

Whatever happened though, and disturbing as it might be when it happened, it was nothing that he didn't understand, that couldn't be measured and studied and explained. It wasn't the house, wasn't anything external at all, just the dysfunctional workings of his own mind and body.

As he relaxed he heard Ruth's voice, then saw Rob, looking exactly as he'd looked at college. Rob was peering into the handset of a telephone and saying he could see something, and then Alex was staring out at him from inside the handset, Rob seeming far away through the pinholes in the plastic.

He was still conscious enough for a small part of his brain to register what was happening. Hypnagogic hallucinations, not dreams, just the mind's jumbled replaying of the day's events. Sleep would follow soon though, and the dreams would come. It was how they came that mattered.

When he woke it was with a start. The room was still dark around him but something was wrong, something he couldn't quite pin down. He tried to move but couldn't, like he'd suffered some kind of seizure. He wasn't breathing properly either but he was awake, his eyes taking in the shadowy details of the room, his ears picking up the delicate background of the machinery.

A real unease started to creep through him. It wasn't the

paralysis – he recognized that now, sleep paralysis. If he stayed calm it would pass, a few minutes and his body would catch up, his brain sending out the signals to free it from sleep. He'd woken suddenly, that was all, the process dislocated.

But he felt uneasy as he lay there; worse, afraid, and he was wondering why he'd woken up the way he had. His eyes darted around the room, his ears straining, the electrical background somehow blocking everything out now. And then he heard something else and realized, that he'd woken because there was someone in the house.

A footstep on the stair. One of the stairs creaked and it had sounded now. He heard nothing else at first but someone was coming up the stairs. He tried again to move but couldn't, the sleep paralysis still locking him in place, stealing his voice, robbing him of everything but the movement of his eyes.

From where he lay he could see only the upper part of the door frame, even with his eyes wrenched downwards in their sockets, but he looked to the door anyway, dreading that he was right and that a figure would appear there. No one came for what felt like minutes.

But then it happened, not a figure filling the door frame, but a shadow slipping through it, silent, a subtle change in the feel of the room, a smell in the air that he couldn't quite identify, a scent, like fruit.

His chest constricted tightly around him, his eyes searching desperately. She was in the room. It was a girl, he knew that, something about the scent. She was in the room, but out of sight, moving along the far edge of the darkness, closer, that scent growing stronger and loaded with malice, a sickening sweetness.

He tried to call out and couldn't, becoming more terrified because he was prone and helpless, unable to move as she crept closer. And then as he fought for breath he slowly began to sense who she was and what she wanted there.

She'd come for him because of that night ten years ago. She was here, the thing he'd always dreaded, she was here to confront him and there was nothing he could do to help himself. All he could do was lie there and wait, the scent growing stronger, the feeling of her physical presence overwhelming his senses.

His eyes were straining to his left, trying to make out her shape against the pale screen of the window and curtains. He fixed on that square and then it was black, as if he'd closed his eyes, and he knew that she was standing next to the bed, looking over him, and that in a moment he would feel her sit down on the mattress next to him and that he would have to see her face, feel her breath on him, the silent suffocating malice.

He knew this terror, and tried to brace himself against it, too late for anything else. She'd come for him and there was no escape. He'd wronged her, and this was her rightful vengeance.

8

He took the tube from the station to Rob's house but then made a couple of wrong turnings in the walk from the tube station, going back to his *A–Z*, stopping a middle-aged woman, then a young guy, neither of them speaking English.

It was a cold morning but sunny and by the time he finally got to the house he'd worked up a sweat and felt uncomfortable for it. He climbed the two steps to the front door but waited for a second, composing himself again. He could hear music somewhere inside, a radio, and then without warning the door opened.

He turned, expecting to see Rob but finding a girl standing there instead, tall and attractive, long brown hair, tanned and athletic. She was looking at him questioningly but as if impatient for him to speak she said, 'I thought I saw someone come up the steps. Can I help?' She was Australian, her accent fresh and friendly, fitting the way she looked.

He checked the door number again and said, 'I'm here to see Rob Gibson.'

'Oh, right,' she said, sounding pleasantly surprised. 'Yeah, come on in. He's in the kitchen.'

She led him through the house into the kitchen where Rob was sitting at a table working on a laptop, unaware of them at first. He was deeply tanned and looked older, weathered. Alex could just see him cutting a dash as a newspaper correspondent.

The girl turned and smiled at Alex, amused because Rob hadn't noticed them. Maybe he had though, because as he typed and stared at the screen he said, 'Hello, Alex,' and turned only a moment or two after he'd said it, smiling, showing a long pale scar now above his right eyebrow, the perfect finishing touch.

'Hello, Rob.' Alex smiled too and nodded, as if acknowledging the strangeness of seeing each other again after all this time.

The girl laughed and said, 'So is that it? This is the great friend you haven't seen for ten years – the least you can do is give each other a bloody hug.'

Straight-faced, Rob said, 'Alex, meet Rebecca; she's Australian you know.'

'Pleased to meet you.'

She smiled and said, 'Yeah, me too. I'll leave you to it.' She gave Rob a knowing smile and walked back out, a door closing on the room where the radio was playing.

Alex waited till she'd gone and said, 'Girlfriend?'

'Only known her a fortnight,' said Rob. 'It's a complicated arrangement. She's my lodger but came through a friend of a friend. I didn't meet her until I came back from Africa. Nice girl though.'

'Yeah, seems nice enough.'

Rob got up and shook Alex's hand and said, 'Have you had no sleep or have you just aged really badly?'

'Bit of both.'

'Jesus, I'm kidding!'

Alex laughed because Rob's accent sounded briefly Australian, a hint of why there seemed to be so much chemistry between him and the girl.

'Come on, let's go straight to lunch. There's a pub down the road does great food, got a separate dining room.'

Rob popped his head in the door to say bye to Rebecca as they left and then talked about her as they walked along the road, nothing specific, just a general enthusiasm for who she was, a vague frustration too that he was leaving in a couple of days.

Alex was envious somehow, trying to remember the last time he'd been energized like that by meeting someone new: Ruth perhaps, Kate definitely, though that had been six years ago. Listening to Rob he felt void of life, cold, like a part of him had died in the last ten years and he was only noticing now.

It was obscene that he'd allowed his own life to drain away like that. Yet even as he became angry with himself his thoughts were laid over a background hiss, a faint voice, whispering, irrational but persistent, that he hadn't allowed it, that his life was being drained from him night by night, a process beyond his control: justice.

Justice. He thought of Will and wondered when Rob would finally mention it. He seemed to be talking about anything but, an odd aversion considering some of the things he'd witnessed and written about during his time in Africa. Possibly he found this more difficult because it was personal. Possibly he just didn't know what to say.

They'd ordered their food when Alex finally broached the subject.

'You seemed uncomfortable talking about Will on the phone yesterday.'

Rob nodded, thinking about it before he said, 'Partly force of habit. I haven't spoken about that night since college. Not once.'

'Me neither, except to Will, but even then, I always tried to steer him away from it. He used to go round in circles, over and over the same things, the what ifs.'

'Didn't we all?' Rob smiled awkwardly and said, 'The other thing is, I wasn't particularly shocked. If it had been you or Matt or Natalie, I wouldn't have believed it, but Will always had it in him to be pushed over the edge. All that business with his family.'

'What business with his family?' Alex didn't remember and yet felt like he should, like it was something he knew, the same family who hadn't wanted their son's belongings.

Rob frowned like he was confused and said, 'Have you had a knock on the head? Will's family were bastards. Politics, law, all that business?'

It came back to him fully formed and he felt bad now for needing to be reminded. He was embarrassed too at the thought of how he'd distanced himself from Will over the years, someone who'd probably needed all the friendship he could have got.

'Of course. It's amazing that I didn't remember that.'

'You got that right. Well, that's what I'm saying anyway. He was a sensitive guy with an horrendously mean family. I'm not denying the accident was the catalyst, but Will was always gonna fall.'

It was the truth that Rob was reminding him of here. Will had been heading towards the comfort of drugs long before the night of the accident, his life so hemmed in by his family that the only way out was through extremes. If it hadn't been the accident it would have been something else that had broken him.

'His flatmate thinks he was murdered,' said Alex, the shift in the discussion so abrupt that Rob looked momentarily confused, as if he'd misheard. 'That's why I wanted to see you, to let you and the others know.'

'To let us know what?'

'Just that. Don't get me wrong, I'm pretty well certain he wasn't murdered, but given the slight possibility that he was, well, I thought it only fair to warn the rest of you, in case we're in danger too.'

Rob was looking at him now as if he'd spoken in tongues, his face paralysed in an expression of stunned confusion.

'Wait there,' he said finally, 'I'm not quite sure I'm getting this. If he *was* murdered, why would that suggest the rest of us were in danger? I don't see a link.'

Alex nodded, feeling slightly embarrassed, his paranoia exposed.

'There probably isn't a link. And it probably was just a straightforward overdose.' He hesitated a second, putting his own thoughts in order, thinking through the best way to present this without sounding like a flake. 'The flatmate brought me his papers, things that Will's family didn't want. There was a scrapbook that he used to keep cuttings in, mainly the cuttings about the accident. Like I said, he was obsessed. Well anyway, the flatmate was convinced that the scrapbook was taken the same weekend Will died, and that it was the only thing stolen.'

Rob was drawn on to a different track for a second, as he said, 'Do you think the flatmate knew why the scrapbook was so important?'

'Maybe. Put it this way, he was scared, too scared to stay in Brighton afterwards. And if the scrapbook *was* taken . . .'

Rob laughed and said, 'I can see where you're coming from here, Alex, but, Jesus, do you honestly think that's likely? No one would go to that much trouble, and besides, why would anyone? We have to assume none of us has talked.'

'We can't assume that. Like we've just said, with Will alone we can't assume that.'

'Okay, true, though even if one of us had talked, it's hard to see how that would lead to something like this. And otherwise, what are we looking at here? We're looking at one of us. Let's face it, we turned out to be a pretty dysfunctional group of friends, and, yeah, we were conceited and generally horrendous people back then, but I don't think any of us were murderer material.'

'I know.' He felt stupid. 'It's not even like there's a possible motive.'

Their food arrived, distracting them momentarily, Alex not even sure if the subject had been dropped altogether. After they'd started eating though, Rob paused, putting down his knife and fork as he said, 'Of course, you're wrong about the lack of a possible motive. I don't think for a second that this has anywhere to go in terms of explaining Will's death, but there was always a fatal flaw in our decision to keep the secret.'

'You're right, I remember Will saying something at graduation.' Will, who despite everything had been effortlessly smarter than the rest of them.

'So do I, about how this could be potentially damaging in the future. See, at the time, once we decided to keep it a secret we all had the same to lose from that secret being revealed, and that's how we always thought it would be. But what if someone suddenly has more to lose than the others?'

He went back to his food, the question left hanging in the air. Alex thought it over, backing away from his own fears, realizing how unlikely it was now that any of the five of them would have so much to lose that they'd consider killing the others. And the idea that it was a revenge killer, that had always seemed absurd.

'Like you said, Will was always gonna fall. It just gets to me,

I suppose, that we weren't there for him. You know, we made a mistake, we did something wrong, but it wasn't like we meant to hurt anyone, so why did it have such an effect?'

Rob smiled, finishing what was in his mouth, taking a gulp of wine, not responding even then but collecting his thoughts instead.

'I don't know. Maybe underneath the veneer of easy success we were all screwed up anyway, or maybe we'd just been so cosseted our whole lives we didn't know how to cope with it. A death, it's quite something to deal with. Ultimately that was our problem: we were shallow, just not shallow enough.' Alex laughed, and then Rob added, 'Anyway, at least you've answered something that's always puzzled me.'

'What?'

'Why you went into the field you did. It seemed a strange choice to me, but from what you just said, I'm guessing you have a personal interest.'

Alex gave a small acknowledging nod and said, 'I don't think I've had a normal night's sleep since it happened.'

'Jesus! Seriously?' Alex nodded and Rob said in disbelief, 'Ten years?'

Alex nodded again, saying, 'Insomnia mainly, but that's almost better than what happens when I sleep. I study sleep paralysis, lucid dreaming, the deep end of nightmares to put it in layman's terms. I explain the patterns of sleep that surround them and I drench them in science. And if I'm truthful, I do it all in an attempt to convince myself that Emily Barratt isn't haunting me, because she does, like she's always there, waiting to catch me off guard.'

'Fuck,' said Rob, his voice quiet with astonishment.

'And what about you?'

Rob didn't answer, looking shocked still, as if his memory of who Alex was had just shattered, the reality spilt before him now and making no sense. 'Sorry, what?'

'I said what about you? I'm guessing the same, that it's affected you in some way.'

'I suppose so,' he said and took another gulp of wine, still looking like someone struggling to move on with the conversation. 'But, Christ, not like that.'

Alex wasn't convinced and said, 'You don't think, at a subconscious level, you might have been drawn to all this horror by a desire to bury what happened in the past?'

'Fuck, no.' He looked baffled by the whole argument. 'Alex, that girl . . .'

'Emily Barratt.'

'Okay, Emily Barratt. She ran in front of our car, bounced off it, bang. I'm happy to admit it was one hell of a shock. I wish it hadn't happened. And I'm sure we all reacted to it differently, but for me, personally, it wasn't a life-changing experience.'

Alex still looked disbelieving and said, 'You're saying it played no part whatsoever in your decision to go into this line of work?' Rob frowned and Alex countered before he could even argue his point. 'I know you always intended to be a journalist. I'm talking about the kind of places you go, things you cover.'

'You do what you do,' said Rob, sounding dismissive. 'Okay, it must have had an effect on me but who knows what it was? Maybe it gave me a taste for it, showed me how raw life could be. And, Jesus, you know, it wasn't that bad. I've had afternoon tea with a guy who sawed off his opponent's ears on live television, and you think I should have nightmares because a girl threw herself in front of a car in which I was a passenger. You know, Alex . . .' He stopped and shook his head, as if unsure whether to proceed.

'Say what you were gonna say.'

Rob weighed it up for a second or two, saying then, 'From what I hear, you've done really well. I'm not knocking that. I wonder how healthy it is, that's all. I mean, you were only a passenger too – there's no way you should have let this fuck up your whole life.'

'Maybe I shouldn't. Who's to say?' Rob shrugged and they ate in silence for a second or two. Alex was desperate to change the subject now, feeling vulnerable, and after casting around for another subject he said, 'Tell me about Natalie.'

'Natalie,' said Rob, as if trying to sum up her decade in the sound of her name alone. 'Of course, Natalie had something else to deal with after leaving college.'

'She left me,' said Alex, his tone too defensive.

'I see you remember that! She left you geographically. I get the impression the reality was a little more complicated.' Alex deferred with a shrug, sensing the uneasy resonance, the way Natalie's name could probably be substituted by Kate's and the statement still hold true. 'Anyway, her career path in the City's been pretty stellar. Okay, she's a workaholic as far as I can tell, but, no kidding, she's left us in the dust.'

Alex nodded. He wanted to ask if she was seeing anyone, married, whatever, but he didn't want to sound like he was still curious. He didn't think Rob would know things like that anyway so he drew a line under it, saying, 'Which leaves Matt. And he wasn't just a passenger.'

Rob looked puzzled for a second, as if he couldn't understand why Alex was still coming back to the accident. He appeared to go along with it then and said, 'Yeah, who knows about Matty? He seemed to take it bad at the time, but he'll have been okay. These patrician American families, they have a way of dealing with things like this.' He laughed then, adding, 'I lay money that if one of us is killing the others, it's Matt, probably getting rid of the skeletons before he runs for office.' Alex looked intrigued, confused for a second, hearing the words and not the sentiment. 'Jesus, Alex, I'm kidding! This is Matt we're talking about. I'm kidding!'

'I know, I know.' He shook his head, amazed at himself. 'It's good speaking to you, Rob. It's been a weird couple of days, you know, some strange little hippy guy arriving in the middle of the night, telling me that Will's dead and that my house has bad vibes, a couple of episodes in my sleep, the whole thing. I haven't been thinking particularly straight.'

'You don't say.' He stared into Alex's eyes for a second or two and smiled, a smile that was edged with regret. 'We made a mistake ten years ago. A crazy woman ran in front of our car and we didn't have the courage to come forward and say just that, make our case. If we had, we'd have lived different lives these last ten years, some of us better, some of us worse, and we wouldn't have lost perspective the way we did. We did nothing wrong. Will died of an overdose. What else is there to say?'

'You're right. Nothing.' Alex showed a renewed interest in the plate of pasta in front of him, changing the subject a minute later. 'So tell me about the scar.'

Rob laughed and said, 'Ask me when I'm pissed – the explanations get better with every drink. Sober, I'm inclined to tell the truth. I fell off a bike in Durban, drunk as, not even my bike.'

Alex encouraged him with questions, enjoying the chance to hear Rob telling yarns, most of them involving drink or narrow escapes from death, a few of them involving both, almost like a caricature of an overseas correspondent's life.

They went back to the house afterwards and had coffee with

Rebecca who wanted to know about their time at college, about Rob, the curiosity of someone who'd made a connection and was hungry to know everything about him. It didn't make Alex sad this time, happy instead at seeing two people with fresh chemistry.

And it made him happy to be talking about college, not about that one night but about the rest of the three years, him and Rob laughing and joking like the intervening years had never happened, their own connection surprisingly intact. Maybe their friendship had been more durable than they'd given it credit for.

That in itself raised a question though, a question that Rebecca finally asked, focusing their attentions immediately back on to the elephant that was sitting in the middle of all those memories, something even Rob couldn't deny.

She shook her head, still smiling from a story Rob had told, and said then, 'The thing I don't understand is why you haven't seen each other in ten years. Okay, life gets in the way but, guys, ten years! I mean, how come?'

Rob looked at Alex before turning to her as he said, 'Sometimes you don't realize what you've got until you let it slip through your fingers. You think you'll make other friends and you do. I've made plenty of friends, but this' – he gestured towards Alex – 'this is like a family reunion to me. We keep in touch from now on, okay?'

'Definitely,' said Alex, though he was wondering how likely that would be, for all the best intentions.

When he was leaving, Rob walked out with him and even to the end of the street, pointing him in the right direction, and just before they parted Alex said, 'So you don't think there's any need to let the others know about this?'

'I'll give Nat a call, tell her about Will. I'll leave it at that though. Seriously, Alex, if I thought there was even the slightest chance that the rest of us were in danger I'd tell her, but there isn't.' He laughed and added, 'Well, except me of course, I'm always in danger.'

Alex said, 'This Kosovo thing isn't likely to be dangerous, is it? I mean, not like Bosnia.'

Rob laughed again. 'More chance of being killed here than I have in Kosovo. Yeah, there's always some danger.' He stopped, like something had suddenly occurred to him. 'Alex, I know we agreed to keep this secret, but it wouldn't do any harm for you to speak to a shrink or someone. It's fucking your life up; you need to talk it through with someone who can help.'

'If it was that simple or straightforward I'd consider it. It isn't though, trust me.'

Rob deferred with a shrug but said, 'Well at the very least, you need a holiday. Chill out. Stop letting life get to you.'

Alex smiled, conscious that he'd sounded like someone who worried too much, someone always scouring the shadows. Maybe that was who he was. It made him realize too, how Rob had changed, how he was calmer now, easier company.

'Don't get killed, Rob, not even drunk on a stolen bike. I need you not to get killed.'

'I'll do my best,' he said, smiling and putting a hand on Alex's shoulder before turning and walking back up the street. Alex watched him for a short while, his figure blurring in the watery afternoon sun as he got further away, and he knew Rob was right, that he needed a holiday, to shed his paranoia, to put flesh back on the bones of who he was.

9

There were no attacks for the next three nights. He put it down to the fact that Rob had reassured him, perhaps even that meeting Rob again had helped him draw a psychological line under his own need to torment himself, under his guilt.

She came again on the fourth night though, and for several nights after that, episodes so disturbing that he had trouble shaking them off during the daylight hours. He was reduced to a state of constant half-sleep, his appearance worrying enough that Ruth couldn't bring herself to joke about it.

On the morning after the third attack she seemed subdued, not in the mood to talk much about anything, occasional looks of concern in his direction as they drank their coffee. He was happy when she left for home, leaving him to go through the backlog of mail that had piled up over the last couple of days.

He'd almost finished when the phone rang, the departmental secretary at the other end.

'Hello, Dr Stratton. I was checking you were still here; there's someone to see you.'

'I'm not seeing students at the moment, Margaret.'

'No, it's personal business. William Shaw.'

Alex's heart kicked out an extra beat and he said, 'Did you say it's about William Shaw?'

'No, it's William Shaw here to see you. Shall I send him round?'

'Yes. Thank you, Margaret.' He put the phone down, struggling to focus his mind, the thoughts running away from him before he could latch on to them. Will was dead, that was the only thing he could fix upon. There was a knock on the door and he said, 'Come in!'

His head began to clear then as a man in his fifties walked into the room, wearing a suit, a smart overcoat. Alex stood up, feeling unsteady. The man's hair was silver, something slightly different about his face too, but even so, Alex understood because he could see now that this was Will's father.

Mr Shaw smiled a little and said, 'I do apologize for dropping in unannounced like this, Dr Stratton. I was visiting the university and I knew you worked here, and that you knew Will. I hope you don't mind me taking the liberty?'

Alex shook his head, saying, 'I'm sorry about your son, Mr Shaw.'

He took a deep breath, relieved as he said, 'Oh, you know about it; that's something of a weight off. And thank you.'

Alex's thoughts were still garbled but in a different direction now. He didn't know how to deal with the man standing in front of him, based on what little he knew of him, what Will had thought of him. He was uneasy too about what might have brought him here.

'Sorry, please take a seat. Would you like a coffee, or tea?'

'No, thank you.' Alex had gestured towards the easy chairs but Mr Shaw sat in the chair on the other side of the desk so the two of them were facing each other as if in a formal interview.

Mr Shaw looked forlorn but dignified and Alex had to remind himself that this was a man who'd helped to destroy his own son, not intentionally perhaps, but that made it no less a cruelty. Most, if not all of Will's weaknesses had been caused by this man and yet he probably had no idea.

'So what can I do for you?'

'Yes, I'm sorry. I'm on my way north and took the opportunity of calling in to see Dr Holborn in the Politics Department. I'm setting up a scholarship in Will's name, to pay for
someone each year to study for a Master's degree.' Alex began
to feel queasy, partly because his memory of Will's relationship with his family was still coming back to him as Mr Shaw
spoke, partly just because of the hollowness of what the man
was talking about. Alex made a show of looking puzzled and
Mr Shaw responded by saying, 'Of course. I wanted to let you
know about his overdose. I didn't know whether any of his
friends knew. I didn't know even to what extent he was still in
touch with all of you.'

'We'd drifted apart,' said Alex.

Mr Shaw nodded. 'I also wanted to ask your opinion, if you
thought there might be some more fitting memorial to Will's
life. As well as the scholarship, of course.'

Alex felt angry, as though he were being asked to condone
the payment of blood money. 'I don't know, Mr Shaw. How
do you remember the life of someone whose spirit was so
comprehensively crushed?' He looked stunned by the
response and Alex immediately regretted saying it, criticizing
a man who, for all his faults, had lost a son just a few weeks
before. 'I'm sorry, I didn't mean that. Er, I think the scholarship is a great idea. He loved his subject.'

Mr Shaw gave a polite smile and said, 'I admire your loyalty
to your friend, and you're quite right of course, painful as it is
to hear.' Alex tried to apologize again but Mr Shaw stopped
him with a small gesture of the hand. He took a deep breath
then, as if composing himself, and said, 'I don't know whether
you ever knew, but Will was older than his brother and sisters
by some five years.'

'No, I didn't.'

'Yes, we moved to South Africa just after he was born and put off having more children until we returned to England. So he was an only child for the four years we were there.' For a moment he looked overwhelmed by the memory, but rallied, smiling as he said, 'It was a very happy time. But when the other children were born, I think we began to demand more of him, and I also freely admit that our expectations were very traditional, very constricting, particularly for someone of Will's temperament. I look at photographs of that beautiful carefree little boy in South Africa, and I think you used the right words, we crushed his spirit.' His eyes looked moist but his voice was clear and steady.

'You can't blame yourself,' said Alex, falling back on cliché.

Mr Shaw looked nonplussed though, and said, 'Why not? That's the trouble with society today: everyone wants to blame someone else, but who else am I to blame? I realized ten years ago that this was my doing.' He laughed a little. 'I was furious at his graduation, because he'd humiliated us, because of the lie, and it took me six months to realize, how terrible it must have been for him that he'd felt that need to lie. I tried to reconcile, of course, more than once, but quite understandably . . .' He trailed off.

'I'm sorry,' said Alex, feeling now like he was the one expressing hollow sentiments.

Mr Shaw smiled and said, 'I should be the one apologizing; I didn't mean to burden you with all of this, and Will is still more deserving of your sympathy than I am.' Alex nodded and he added, 'And at least I have some consolation, that I was given the chance to avoid the repetition of my mistakes.'

'I don't follow.'

'My other children. Lucy was sixteen when Will graduated, Sam was fourteen, Georgie only eleven. Thankfully, the upheaval of that summer removed the scales from my eyes just in time. It's enough to have one thwarted life on your conscience – I don't think I could have borne all four.'

Alex nodded but suddenly began to feel uncomfortable. Here was a man who'd unwittingly wronged his own son but who'd acknowledged that failure and sought to atone. Alex had condemned him on sight and yet he didn't even have the right to judge him, not when he'd made a journey of redemption like that.

'Why didn't you want his letters, his notebooks?'

Mr Shaw looked confused for a second, perhaps wondering how Alex had known about it, but then he said, 'We looked through them. They spoke, to me, of the lifestyle that killed him. I'm not a masochist, Dr Stratton. I want to remember who he was, not what he became.'

'So you didn't keep anything from the flat in Brighton?'

'As I remember it, there wasn't anything else to keep.'

'Of course,' said Alex, thinking of this well-dressed man, his wife, perhaps one or more of his other children, looking lost and helpless in a bare and cold flat, trying to take on board the truth of how far Will had run from them. 'I didn't mean to intrude on your grief, and I'm sorry, I had no right to make the comments—'

'You had every right.'

Alex avoided looking at him but said, 'The scholarship is a nice idea. If I think of anything else, I'll let you know.'

'Thank you,' said Mr Shaw and handed him a business card.

He got up then and Alex stood with him.

'I'll walk you to your car. Where are you parked?'

'The visitor parking by the Chaplaincy Centre, but, really, there's no need.'

'I'd like to.'

Mr Shaw asked about the others as they walked. Alex told him about Rob, what little he knew of Natalie, admitting then that he knew nothing of what Matt was doing. He was surprised too that Mr Shaw knew who these people were, that Natalie had been Alex's girlfriend, that Matt came from New York.

'There was another girl,' said Mr Shaw then. 'Lara? Laura?'

Alex tried to think who he could be talking about, drawing a blank, saying finally, 'Not that I remember, certainly not one of our group.'

Mr Shaw nodded and smiled, looking around as he said, 'I think he was very happy here. I take a lot of comfort in that.' He pointed to a Jaguar parked across the road from them. There was a girl sitting in the passenger seat and she got out as they approached and smiled. She looked like a student and Alex guessed it was Will's youngest sister.

'Georgie, this is Dr Alex Stratton, Will's friend.' The words grated but the girl smiled and shook his hand, said hello.

She looked at her father then, her smile tinged with concern as she said, 'Are you okay?'

He smiled back at her, a look of reassurance. 'Yes, I'm fine.' He turned to Alex and said, 'Thank you, I enjoyed our talk.'

'Me too. I'm glad I had the chance to meet you.'

Alex saw them off, standing in the winter sunshine long after the car had disappeared, left dwelling on the affection there'd been between father and daughter, and on the things Mr Shaw had said in his office. The whole experience had left him feeling ashamed.

He thought then of the other girl he'd mentioned, wondering now if he'd got the name completely wrong, if perhaps it hadn't been Lara or Laura, but Emily. And thinking of her, he realized he was standing only a few hundred yards from a bench that had been bought in her memory, the synchronicity sending him off in that direction.

It had been bought with a collection raised by friends in her college, situated now in front of a small thicket of trees, looking down over the landscaped campus to the lake and the woods beyond, a thin silvery line of sea above them in the distance.

He went there maybe once a year, drawn by the need to reread the inscription that told him just a little of who she was, or, rather, who she'd been. This seemed like as good a time as any and he sat huddled against the chill wind, looking out at the view for ten minutes or so before turning to look at the weather-dulled plaque.

Emily Barratt, nineteen, only nineteen when she died, still a month short of her twentieth birthday. And there were the mawkish words with which her friends had tried to capture her essence, for all the people who would sit on this bench in the future and wonder who she was: 'an angel walked among us'.

Perhaps her friends would have been embarrassed ten years on to remember what they'd written in a heightened state of grief, but, even so, it spoke of someone good and gentle, someone who shouldn't have died, not the furious angel who'd infiltrated his own mind.

That was how she'd looked too, ten years before. It was hard to remember now, but that brief glimpse had been of someone angelic, like the angels he remembered from da Vinci paintings. And yet it was a face that his subconscious had twisted and filled with spite and malevolence.

He turned again and looked at the view. Two female students were walking slowly along one of the paths up the hill, cutting diagonally across his vision before disappearing to his right. They were a long way off but he could hear them talking as they walked, laughing occasionally, carefree.

It was a strange place to have a memorial, a university campus, a place where nothing ever changed, where history was simultaneously repeated and airbrushed in an unchanging three-yearly cycle. The students walking the hill below him knew nothing of the people who'd left three months before their own arrival, let alone three years, ten years, more.

But here was a memorial bench, a reminder of a dead person who no one here remembered. And despite that, it was still comforting somehow, the thought that strangers might sit here to enjoy the view and be moved for even a second or two to think about who she might have been.

He imagined a similar plaque bearing Will's details. There'd be no sugary epitaph, and anyone studying it would see that he hadn't died so young, but they'd still be given cause to wonder, who he'd been, how he'd died, why someone had cared enough about him to want him remembered.

Despite everything Alex had imagined though, the people who cared about Will were his family, not the friends who'd thought nothing of marking his life. And he felt guilty, because Will's father blamed himself for his son's slide into heroin, and yet the blame should have been aimed just as much at his friends, people who'd forced him into a straitjacket ten years before and then abandoned him.

He got up and headed back, not towards his own department but to the Alumni Office. He didn't know why he hadn't thought of it before, but he was determined now that Will should have a memorial and that he should pay for it himself, a tree perhaps rather than a bench, a distinction Will would have appreciated.

He'd pay for a tree, something to mark Will's passing, and in the process he'd ease his own mind of any sense that he'd done too little to help someone he should have helped. It was a memorial though, he kept telling himself that, not a talisman to ward off his own guilt but a memorial.

When he got to the Alumni Office he found two women sitting at computers, one of them in her early twenties, looking like she'd been a student herself fairly recently. They looked expectantly at him, a warmth that somehow suggested they saw him as a visitor to be welcomed, not one of the residents.

He said hello and then, 'I want to pay for a tree to be planted, for a former student who died.'

'Oh,' said the younger one, looking puzzled.

The older woman, probably no older than him now that he looked at her, began to search through papers on her desk and said, 'Yes, I've got a note somewhere with the name of the person you need, someone in Estates I think.' She seemed to become distracted then and said, 'While we're at it, maybe I could make a note of your friend's name? We'll amend the records and include him on our memorial page.'

'William Shaw.' She tapped the name into the computer.

Alex started to give extra information, his graduation year, college, but she looked up with a mildly patronizing smile and said, 'It's okay, I have him.' She busied herself for a second, telling her computer that William Shaw need no longer be invited to reunions or asked for donations. Then she screwed up her face slightly and said, 'What a coincidence. That's two deaths we've heard about this week and they're both from the same year.'

'How sad,' said the younger woman, like they were talking about old men. 'I wonder if they knew each other.'

'I suppose they might well have done. It makes you stop and think, doesn't it, how you never know what a day might bring?'

'True,' said the younger one, her expression lost somewhere between thoughtful and vacant.

Alex continued to stand there, listening to them talking to each other as if he wasn't even in the room with them. He felt light-headed, his chest tightening. He wanted to ask who the other person was but was unable to, and not even sure if he wanted to hear it.

Rob had persuaded him that nothing was wrong, that Will had died of an overdose, that it had always been on the cards, that it was ludicrous to suggest any other explanation. And it *was* ludicrous but he had an uneasy feeling that he would ask for a name and it would be Matt or Natalie. How would Rob explain it then?

'Are you okay? Would you like to sit down?'

Alex looked at the younger woman and said, 'I'm fine, thanks.' She was looking at him like he was drunk. He turned to the other woman and said, 'The other person.'

'You know Robert Gibson,' she said, 'the journalist?'

'I mean, the other person who died. Who was it?'

'Robert Gibson,' she said, irritated at having to repeat herself.

Alex laughed, a laugh that seemed to put a strain on his heart, clawing the muscle. The woman looked disgusted now but Alex said, 'You don't understand, I had lunch with Rob Gibson last week in London. So clearly, you're mistaken.'

'I think *you* must be mistaken,' she said, patience fraying. 'The Robert Gibson I'm talking about was a reporter in Kosovo so I find it highly unlikely that you would have been having lunch with him in London.'

He said something but couldn't be sure what it was. Maybe

it had been nothing intelligible because the woman's annoyance was edged with confusion now. And he felt drunk himself, his balance, his perception of space, the whole world distorting, retreating from him.

He felt himself fall, the slow creaking fall of a large tree expertly felled. He couldn't see anything as he collapsed, could hear only a distant version of the woman speaking. Something crashed against the side of his head and the woman in the distance asked him desperately what he thought he was doing.

When he came round, both of the women were looking at him, concerned now. 'He's coming round,' the younger one said, and he smiled, a response that seemed to increase the look of anxiety on their faces. It took him a moment to realize he was on the floor and they were looking down at him, crouched either side of his body, a moment more to take in that the side of his head hurt badly.

'Are you okay? I think you fainted.'

'I'm fine. I think I hurt my head.'

The older woman glanced at the side of his head, grimacing slightly as she said, 'You caught the edge of the desk as you fell. It's not bleeding but it's already swollen.'

'Like an egg,' said the other one.

'Can you get up?'

'I think so.' He got slowly to his feet, the two women guiding him up without really helping him, then moving him backwards into a chair.

'I'll get you some water,' said the younger one and left the room. He lifted his hand and touched the bump just behind his temple, disturbingly like an egg, just like she'd said.

'I'm sorry about this,' Alex said.

The older woman looked regretful herself and said, 'Don't

be silly.' She paused then before adding, 'So I gather you knew Robert Gibson?'

He closed his eyes, remembering what had brought on the fainting fit or whatever it was. The concept of Rob being dead still jarred. Will's death hadn't shocked him but Rob had been too full of life, too recently.

'I had lunch with him. He's only been in Kosovo a few days.'

'He was hit by mortar fire. He was taking cover with another journalist and the building they were in was hit by a mortar shell. They were both killed. It was in the paper, the day before yesterday I think.' He opened his eyes again and she smiled helplessly. 'How awful that you've lost two friends so close together.'

He nodded and then the younger woman came back in with cup of water. She gave it to him but stared at the side of his head rather than making eye contact.

'Thanks.'

He sipped at the water, warm and tasting of dust, as the older woman said, 'This gentleman knew Robert Gibson. That's two of his friends have died.'

'How awful,' she said.

'Did it say anything about the funeral?'

She looked pleased with herself. 'You know, I'm glad you d about that, because it didn't, but I made a point of ng out, just in case anyone needed to know. You should s make the Alumni Office your first stop.' She sounded meone trying to justify the existence of her own job. She looked through the papers on her desk again and said, 'It's at eleven thirty next Tuesday, in St Bride's, Fleet Street, you know, where they have the memorial services for journalists.'

The younger one said to her colleague, 'I expect we'll have a memorial service for him here. After all, he wrote for Times.'

'He wrote for The *Daily Telegraph*,' said Alex, the two them looking at him for a second and then looking away again Thinking of Natalie and Matt now, he added, 'I wonder, do you have any details for Matt MacAndrew and Natalie Ha' rison from the same year? I really should let them know ab this but I don't have any up-to-date addresses.'

The two women looked at each other before the olde said, 'We can't give out people's details to anyone who asl them.'

'Not even to a member of staff?'

'Well, if you were a member of staff we'd have to consider the request on its merits.'

He touched his head again, probing tentatively at the delicate surface of the bump.

'I am a member of staff. I'm Dr Alex Stratton, from the Psychology Department.'

'Are you the sleep person?' It was the younger woman suddenly interested, and when he nodded she said, 'Ho interesting. I have the strangest dreams. I've often wonder about them.'

'Really?' He turned to the other woman and said, 'So?'

'I'm afraid not. You see, you've made clear yourself that want their details for personal, not professional reasons. W simply not allowed to divulge information like that; it's law.'

He wanted to be able to tell her that these people might be in danger but he couldn't, saying instead, 'Even under these circumstances?'

'I'm afraid so. I really am sorry and I wish I could help you but the rules are the rules.'

'I'll tell you what, can you at least tell me if their addresses have been updated since graduation? That won't contravene any law, will it?'

She weighed it up, a look of suspicion as if she thought she was being duped somehow, but then she walked back behind her desk and said, 'What were the names again?'

'Matthew MacAndrew and Natalie Harrison.'

She typed into the computer and sat in silence for a while, saying finally, 'Their addresses haven't been updated since leaving. That doesn't mean they're still there, just that they've never contacted us.'

'Thank you.' He handed the cup back and got to his feet, the two of them looking as nervous as if he'd been setting out across a tightrope.

'Are you sure you're okay?'

'I'm fine, really, and thanks again.' He turned and walked out, stopping at the door to say to the younger woman, 'You should write them down.'

'I'm sorry?'

'Your dreams; you should write them down.'

'Oh. Thank you.' He smiled, not sure what she was thanking him for, and walked across the square to the library.

He never usually had much call to be in there and being there now reminded him of his student days, an evocative recollection that weighed him down. He went into the journals room and scanned the week's newspapers, his attention caught not by a headline but by a picture of Rob taken the day before his death.

There he was, a couple of days after their lunch, three days ago, laughing with a drink in his hand, like he was talking to Alex off the page. It seemed like a magician's trick that he was dead, as if the sleight of hand would suddenly be revealed and Rob would tap him on the shoulder and explain the illusion.

Even the story read like something he'd seen before. Rob had been in a deserted smallholding with a Dutch journalist when it had come under fire. They'd taken shelter in a barn which had been hit by a mortar or artillery shell. Rob had been killed instantly. The Dutch journalist had died of his wounds on the way to the hospital.

Alex stared at the page, imagining how Will probably would have cut carefully around the article and pasted it in his scrapbook. Perhaps he'd have rearranged things too, so that the story about Rob was next to the stories about Emily Barratt, like they were part of the same investigation. Except, of course, the stories about Emily Barratt had disappeared with the scrapbook.

He shook his head, trying to make sense of all the strange drift washing up around him, whether it was unrelated or whether all the pieces together would point to some single tragedy far out at sea. The trouble was, even on their own the pieces seemed unbelievable, like none of this was real, like he'd imagined it all.

He got up and headed out. As he walked towards the lobby he saw two students walking towards him, a boy and girl. She smiled a little at him but then looked concerned and slowed, somehow managing to bring him to a stop with her body language.

'Wow, Dr Stratton, what happened to your head?' He looked puzzled and she said, 'Emma Darling, I did your course last year, Psychology 216.'

'Strangely, not only do I remember the name of my own course, I also remember you, Miss Darling.' He realized his tone was wrong, coming across pompous and sarcastic, leaving her slightly humiliated. He heard himself speak sometimes and wondered what had happened to him. 'You wrote a good piece on post-traumatic dreams. I gave you a first for it.'

She smiled, bashful, and then pointed at his head. 'That looks really nasty.'

'It's nothing, really. It looks much worse than it is.' She didn't look convinced. 'So you're in your final year now?' She nodded and he said, 'Well, best of luck.'

'Thank you.' She still looked concerned but touched too, Alex happy that he'd managed to redeem himself for once, make himself seem vaguely normal, human. Even so, he noticed the guy looking on with a bemused expression, probably itching to say something as soon as they walked away.

Alex even turned and looked after them as they headed towards short loan. They looked good together, and as he watched them he thought briefly of Natalie. Sometimes it seemed so recent, and he couldn't work out how he'd transformed from one of those kids walking away into the person he was now; the time had been too short, the change too great.

He walked back to his car but when he got there he just sat for a while studying the bump in the passenger mirror. It looked pretty nasty, like a deformity, the part of it that wasn't covered by his hair already beginning to bruise up badly. He felt okay but now that he'd seen it he decided to sit there for a while before driving home.

He thought about Rob, not so much about the fact he was dead, but what he might have said about his own death. Almost certainly he'd have put it down to chance, a regular roll of the dice in a war zone, and it was hard to imagine how it could have been anything else.

Two of Alex's friends had died within the space of a few weeks, both in ways that appeared unfortunate but both a long way from being suspicious. If they hadn't had the misfortune of being in the same car ten years before Alex would never have given it a second thought himself.

And if anything, it made him more determined that Rob had been right. Faking a drug overdose was one thing, plausible enough, but arranging to have someone blown up by a local militia in a war zone was a different story, the kind of thing only a conspiracy theorist would believe in. The fact was, Matt and Natalie weren't in danger, and certainly neither of them was a killer.

He started the car and pulled away. He needed to get home and eat and have a decent night's sleep. The night ahead was out of his hands but he just felt if he could sleep, long and untroubled and dreamless, he'd begin to see everything in the right perspective, regain his balance again.

An untroubled sleep, not much to ask for but something that seemed beyond him. He woke in the early hours, uneasy at first but then relaxing, realizing he wasn't in the middle of an attack. He was thirsty though, his mouth dry. Perhaps that was why he'd woken.

He got up without turning on the light and made his way downstairs. It didn't matter that it was dark; he knew the way blind, stepping over the creaking stair, wanting to maintain the silence.

And he was glad he hadn't turned on the lights because the downstairs was lit anyway, swimming in the unearthly glow of the streetlights coming in through the front windows. He was surprised they lit up the whole place as much as they did, giving it a strangely atmospheric quality, like a theatre set.

He walked into the kitchen and filled a glass with water. He shivered then, sensing that someone was behind him, the air stirring, like someone had crossed the hall behind him. He turned quickly but saw no one, just the empty orange glow. It felt like someone was there though. Putting the glass down, he walked back through, uneasy.

He looked into the lounge where the light was even brighter. Will was sitting in the armchair cutting things out of newspapers. He looked up briefly and smiled at Alex. Alex nodded back and Will said, 'Why are you crying?'

He put his hand to his eyes, dry, and said, 'I'm not crying. None of this happened.'

Will nodded and went back to his papers. The phone rang and Alex picked it up. There was a lot of noise at the other end, gunfire, distant explosions, and then an urgent voice, 'She's in the house, Alex. She's in the house!'

'Rob?'

'How can it be me? I'm here.' He looked in the direction of the voice. Rob was sitting on the sofa, his face covered with an intricate map of white scars.

'They managed to patch you up,' said Alex.

Rob looked confused and then Alex became aware of the voice screaming in the telephone. He'd let the receiver drop and as he looked down at it now he could hear the desperate screaming, 'She's in the house! She's in the house!'

She was in the house. What did that mean? She was in the house. He felt the sensation again of someone walking past behind him, a swift flitting movement. He looked back out to the hallway, nothing there. And then he heard the stair creak and when he turned again Rob and Will were backing into the corner on the far side of the room, looking afraid, becoming children.

'She's in the house,' said Rob. 'She's always been here.'

'Who?' They covered their mouths and Alex said, 'Wait here,' and climbed the stairs then, emerging in the doorway to his room. The glowing of the streetlights was in there too now, not as bright but well enough to see.

Someone was on the bed with her back to him, someone familiar somehow. He walked closer, realizing that someone else was in the bed too and that she was straddling his chest. He couldn't see what she was doing at first but as he got closer he realized her hands were covering the sleeper's mouth, obscuring his face.

Her own face was hidden too, her hair hanging down, and even as he got closer he couldn't see it. The person under her began to struggle, buckling helplessly, and Alex tried to shout now but couldn't, like there was no air in his lungs.

He got closer, bending down, trying to look at her face, until his head was almost touching hers and still he couldn't see. He reached out and touched her hair and made to brush it back but as his hand moved a sense of dread started to well up inside him. And then without warning she turned quickly and her face was against his, cold, a sickening scream.

'Alex!' He woke violently, sweat-drenched and sprang automatically from the bed, lunging for the light. He fell back on to the edge of the bed, momentarily blinded, his heart punching at his chest, his breath catching in his lungs like he'd been running hard. He felt sick at the realism of the dream, too disconcerted even to reason it through in his mind.

He thought of the final shout then, the shout that had woken him just before he'd seen her face. It seemed likely it was part of the dream and yet it had seemed external. The confusion was enough to make him go over to the window and look down into the street below, emptiness, the black windows of the offices opposite.

He let the curtain go again quickly and turned away. He couldn't go on like this. He had to leave this house, this town, to make at least some initial steps in the direction of leaving himself behind, forging a new existence. He didn't know whether he could escape or not but he knew that as long as he stayed here the past would keep pulling him in like quicksand.

He walked out on to the landing, a relentless ice-water drip shuddering down his spine, and he walked through the house turning the lights on as he went, another shudder as he came to each doorway, each room, each turn. The place was empty, he knew that.

He made his way back upstairs then, sensing someone in the kitchen behind him, telling himself he'd just been in there and it was empty, counter-reason arguing that it often seemed to be the kitchen, as if some force, some presence resided there, the thing Luke had picked up on perhaps. He chastised himself, reminding himself of the truth.

He was a man riddled with guilt, that was all, his thoughts made cancerous by his knowledge of a girl's death and the indirect part he'd played in it. That's what it was, guilt, remorse, feelings he'd nurtured and made his own beyond all reason, seeking even to acquire more of it wherever he could.

The time would come when he'd finally have to face those demons for what they were and deal with them, his word to the others no longer worth the torment that came with keeping the secrets he held. And if things continued as they were, he'd soon be the only one left to hurt from revealing those secrets anyway.

IO

It wasn't far from the tube station, the church set back from the street in a narrow recess, people milling around outside in suits and black ties. A handful of guys who looked like journalists themselves were standing in a huddle, talking in low voices.

Alex stood nearby, none of the others appearing to notice him, certainly not paying him any attention. He was eager to hear what they were talking about, how they thought of Rob, who he'd become in the ten years since they'd known each other.

There were five of them, but two, a young guy and another who looked close to retirement, said nothing, listening instead to the other three who were talking conspiratorially.

As Alex came within earshot one of them said, 'Who was the Dutch guy? Maybe it was him.'

'No, he was a solid straightforward guy, unexceptional. I'm telling you, it was Rob.'

'I'm with Jim. He made a lot of enemies in the establishment. This was payback.'

'Enemies in Africa. And think about it, they could have done this a lot easier out there.'

'Could they? I'm not so sure.'

It took Alex a few seconds to work out what they were saying, a hollowness in his stomach as it sank in, his mind retching broken thoughts. They were talking about Rob's death like it was suspicious: the one thing he'd relied upon as being fanciful.

'You're ignoring something,' said the doubter, 'the mundane but likely scenario that it really was just an accident. Incidents of friendly fire like this happen all the time.'

'So why did it take two days for them to admit it was friendly fire?'

'Because that's the way they are. I think Rob's luck ran out, that's all. And let's face it, it lasted a bloody long time as it was.'

'True enough. Jesus, is that true enough!'

They laughed about that and seemed ready to move on then, but the old guy spoke and they all fell silent, his voice drawling over the words, full of old school authority.

'We'll never know the truth, but frankly, this stinks. Someone wanted our boy Rob dead. Look at the facts. CIA connection gives Rob the nod on this location, evidence of atrocities. There's no activity whatsoever in the area but the Americans decide nevertheless to hit the place with an artillery barrage just after Rob gets there. Thirty minutes of bombardment and then nothing. And was there any evidence of atrocities?' He fastened his collar and straightened his tie. 'Say what you like but this was a sting. Someone used a sledgehammer to crack a walnut, and the walnut was Rob Gibson. We do him a disservice if we don't acknowledge that fact.' He walked slowly away and into the church.

The others looked at each other without saying anything and then started to move too, the younger guy taking his cue from the other three; Alex got the impression that perhaps he alone hadn't known Rob. The other three looked weary with grief, a permanent grief they probably kept to themselves except on occasions like this.

'Excuse me,' said Alex and the three of them turned, a look of surprise as if they really hadn't noticed him standing there. He looked apologetic and said, 'I couldn't help overhearing. You think someone killed Rob intentionally?'

They appeared to close ranks against his question, only the young guy unsure how to react. One of the three who'd been discussing it said, 'We're just speculating.'

'You shouldn't pay too much attention to what journalists say to each other,' said a second, the one who'd played the part of sceptic.

Sensing their defensiveness Alex said, 'It's important that I know. I'm an old college friend of Rob's and, well, another of our circle died in mysterious circumstances recently.'

'I'm sorry to hear that,' said the sceptic. The other two were still looking on suspiciously but he added, 'Look, I can understand your concern but, believe me, even if Rob's death was suspicious, and we have no proof of that, the chances of there being a connection are almost nil.'

One of the other two said now, 'What do you do for a living?'

'I'm an academic, a psychologist. I have nothing to do with this – I just want to be sure that . . .'

He ground to a halt and before he could continue the guy said, 'This doesn't concern you. It doesn't even concern us. Just do yourself a favour and forget that you heard anything. Your friend died in an accident, that's all there is to it.'

Alex wanted to say something, irritated at the way the guy had spoken to him, but he'd turned immediately and walked into the church, his younger colleague hesitating for a second and then following him.

'Sorry about that,' said the sceptic. 'This has been a shock for all of us. He still had no excuse for talking to you like that.'

'It's okay. I understand.'

The other remaining guy smiled a little, regretfully, and said, 'Jim was right though, you should forget about it, otherwise it'll just eat you up, because, believe me, you'll never get to the truth.'

They walked away, leaving Alex on his own, almost amused by their communal advice to forget about it. If it was as easy to do as it was to say his life would be a lot simpler, if less true perhaps. Some things weren't meant to be forgotten.

He checked his watch and followed them into the church, a bright building, clear glass windows, giving it the look of an administrative building rather than a holy place. The pews were facing each other across the aisle but they were full and between them there were rows of additional seats facing forward.

He sat on one of the few empty chairs in a row near the back and took in the congregation, mainly men in suits, more women up near the front, Rob's parents looking the way he remembered them from college. He noticed Rebecca sitting near the front too and thought maybe he'd speak to her afterwards.

Then he noticed the most obvious thing in the place, something that his eyes had still managed to register last, Rob's coffin sitting in front of the altar, looking like part of the church's fittings. It was too unreal, Alex feeling a desperate need to see inside it, to get proof, a need he quickly dismissed as a standard response to grief.

And yet grief itself was an inappropriate word for what he was feeling, his thoughts too internalized and self-absorbed. He wasn't even sure that he felt anything for Rob right now, his death serving only as a device for cranking up the tension another notch in his own claustrophobic little drama.

He looked around at the rest of the congregation, wondering what they felt. Most of them looked emotionally isolated, aware of those around them but locked in a personal struggle, like people treading water at sea after a shipwreck. Only a few seemed to be talking quietly, expressions of disbelief or saddened resignation.

Alex looked at them all and knew he didn't feel what they felt. He felt nervous, afraid even. A part of him was at least concerned for Matt and Natalie but now even that was being tempered by the fear that one of them was behind this, that one of them was eliminating the people who could place them in that car on that night.

The service started but Alex was distracted now, thinking through the logistics, what kind of resources someone would need to kill people in such an extraordinary way. To have killed Will would probably have been within the capabilities of an enthusiastic amateur but Rob's death would have taken a lot of contacts, a lot of power.

And if the same person had killed both of them he was pretty certain it had to be one of the five. Even if some of them had talked in the years since, he couldn't see how it would have got back to someone who might want to avenge Emily Barratt's death. And someone who'd wanted revenge would have had an easier option too: the police, justice.

If the deaths were suspicious they were almost certainly linked to Emily Barratt's death but beyond that the possibilities were limited: a revenge killer or someone who wanted to hush up the past. He knew nothing of her family and he hadn't had much to do with his friends for ten years, but his mind was heading instinctively in one direction only.

It had to be one of the five. And sadly, it had to be Matt. It was a difficult thought to take on board, that the Matt they'd known ten years ago could be responsible for something like this, but it had to be him. The journalists had mentioned the CIA, the friendly fire had come from the US army, and, like Rob himself had said, Matt was the one most likely to be in a position now where he might need to clean up the past like that.

Alex had been going through the motions of the service without paying much attention but a guy got up to read the lesson now, Rob's brother, a physical similarity that was alarming. Alex didn't even remember him having a brother. He began to read, his voice disturbingly similar too, remaining steady and composed.

When he finished and walked away Alex became aware of the guy sitting next to him. He'd been aware of him only as someone in a dark blue suit but he began to sob now, quietly, his head bowed.

Alex turned and looked at him, a guy of around their own age. He thought of saying something but didn't, unsure what to say, and then he noticed that the woman on the other side had put her hand on top of the crying man's, squeezing it gently, reminding him perhaps that he wasn't alone in this.

It seemed a fitting gesture, one that Alex couldn't have offered. He wasn't even sure what he would have said to the man beyond the standard selection of empty condolences. Some people were good to have around in a time of crisis, but he wasn't one of them. He never had been.

When the service ended Alex went with the flow out of the church. Rob's parents and brother were at the door shaking hands with the congregation, thanking them, acknowledging that it was a beautiful service. There were enough people passing through the door though, for Alex to slide past without them even noticing him.

He waited outside where plenty of other people were milling around, talking, letting off the steam of all that dignified and pent-up emotion. He was looking out for Rebecca, wanting to speak to her. He saw her appear in the doorway but she talked to Rob's brother and parents for a few minutes.

He kept watching, only vaguely aware of the other people around him, and then he felt a hand tap him on the shoulder. He turned and stared for a second or two at the woman standing there, a momentary struggle to take in who it was.

'Hello, Alex.' She smiled.

'Hello, Nat.' Her hair was shorter now, and she was slimmer perhaps, or maybe that was just the black business suit playing tricks. Her face was unchanged though, the smile peeling away the years, taking him back immediately to another past, one that wasn't dominated by the death of Emily Barratt.

'It's good to see you,' she said.

He nodded and she hugged him, almost formally at first but clinging tighter to him as he put his arms around her, like she was afraid of falling. It felt good to be held like that, one more part of normal life that he'd lost somewhere along the line, and the way she was holding him made him wonder if she'd lost it too.

When she stood back her eyes were moist. She took a tissue from her bag and dabbed them dry, apologized and said, 'Shall we go for lunch somewhere? Do you have to rush off?'

He looked around, Rebecca still talking to Rob's family. He wasn't sure why he wanted to speak to her anyway. Maybe he'd just wanted to speak to someone without feeling like a fraud.

'No, I don't have to be anywhere. I'd love to have lunch.'

She smiled warmly. 'Good. There's a nice Italian place not far from here. I'm pretty certain they'll find us a table. Come on, we'll walk.'

She linked her arm through his as they walked into the street and the barrage of traffic noise. It was something they'd never done as a couple, linked arms or held hands as they'd walked, and it seemed to speak somehow of all the relationships she'd had since, that this kind of affection no longer seemed mawkish to her.

As if thinking along the same lines, she said, 'Are you seeing anyone?' He laughed and she said, 'What?'

'Nothing,' he said, 'I'm just laughing because I was wondering the same about you.' He turned and smiled at her. 'I don't think I'd have cut quite to the chase like that though.'

She smiled too and said, 'Funny thing about being a single woman, when you reach my age you find yourself being a lot more direct. Not that I'm suggesting we're a potential hookup, by the way. I'm just curious.'

'So you're single?' She nodded. 'Me too.' They walked on for a while in silence and then Alex said, 'Would it be such an horrendous prospect, hooking up with me again?'

'Of course not, but you know . . .' She looked around her and said, 'Cross here,' leading him across the road with a gentle tug on the linked arm. Once they were on the other side and walking again she said, 'You were my first love, Alex, and I'm sure it wasn't perfect – I certainly hadn't planned for it to end when it did – but in my memory, it is perfect. So I don't know, maybe it's best left like that.'

'You always told me that boy in the sixth form was your first love. What was his name, Simon?'

'Stephen,' she said, laughing. 'No, I was never in love with Stephen. I just used to tell you that because . . . Oh, I don't know, because it's the kind of lie you tell when you're young.'

He nodded but didn't respond, his thoughts sent off on a tangent, sinking under the weight of the lies they'd told when they were young. After a while though, he sensed that he'd been silent too long and said, 'I didn't notice you in the church.'

'I know you didn't. I noticed you as soon as you walked in but you seemed very preoccupied. Short of whistling I wasn't sure how to attract your attention.'

'Whistling probably wouldn't have been appropriate.'

'Probably not, though Rob might well have been entertained.' Her arm seemed to tighten slightly in his and her voice sounded constricted as she said, 'It was a beautiful service, wasn't it?'

'I suppose so. To be truthful, I had trouble concentrating on it. I only had lunch with him the other week and I don't think it's quite sunk in yet.'

'So you and Rob have been in touch with each other? He's never mentioned it.'

'That's the irony,' said Alex. 'Lunch the other week was the first time we've seen each other in ten years. We only got together really to talk over what happened to Will.'

'Why, what's happened to him?' He looked at her, checking from her expression what should have been obvious enough, that she didn't know. Rob clearly hadn't found the time to tell her before leaving.

'He's dead.'

She slowed to a halt and let go of his arm, turning to face him. 'Will's dead?' He nodded. 'Was it an overdose?'

'Sadly predictable, but yeah.'

She looked like someone who'd taken a blow to the head, saying finally, 'Jesus, talk about it never fucking rains.' Sidetracked, she said, 'Did you go to his funeral?'

'No. I only found out afterwards.' Though now that he thought of it, he hadn't asked Luke about a funeral, and probably wouldn't have gone anyway, Will's death tainted somehow whereas Rob's had been heroic. It was a false distinction, a superficiality that neither of them would have appreciated, made falser still by the possibility they'd both shared exactly the same kind of death.

'How sad,' said Natalie, sounding touched, as if imagining Will being buried in some desolate pauper's plot without any mourners at all. He thought of mentioning the visit from Will's father but thought better of it, not wanting to muddy the waters.

He simply said, 'I know, I was thinking of paying for a tree to be planted on campus, you know, as a memorial.'

'That's a nice idea.' She thought about it for a second then snapped out of it and pointed at the door behind her. 'This is it.'

'Oh, right.' He followed her in. It was a small busy place but they appeared to recognize Natalie and had no trouble finding them a table tucked away near the back.

The menus were oversized, demanding to be looked at right away, and so they ordered quickly and then once they were left alone again, Natalie smiled and said, 'I've been itching to ask, but what on earth happened to your head?'

He automatically lifted his hand to the bump which had almost disappeared and had lost its tenderness. The bruising still looked angry, an abstract mess of yellow and blue-black. He was about to tell her what had happened but held back, wanting for some reason to maintain his reputation as someone who kept calm in a crisis, feeling it important, particularly now.

'It's a long story,' he said, 'nothing exciting. Suffice to say it involved alcohol.'

She laughed and said, 'You see, that's the danger of staying in academia; you never grow up.'

He laughed too, amused by the picture she had of him now as an eternal student, living it up like adult life had passed him by. It was hard to imagine how she could have been further from the truth.

'It's not all fun and games you know.'

'I know, I've followed your career, I mean, not like in a stalking way, but I know what you've been up to.' He felt guilty that he'd thought of her so rarely over the intervening years, no nagging curiosity, no idle speculation about where she might be or what she might be doing.

'Rob told me you've done pretty well.' She shrugged, downplaying her success.

'What is it you do?'

'I work in the City; it's not particularly interesting. I mean, it's a great job, but . . .'

The waiter brought the wine, distracting them for a short while, and once he'd gone Alex said, 'Look, I may as well get this out of the way now. I don't even know what to think of it myself so I'll just put the facts before you and let you interpret it as you see fit.'

'Well, this all sounds very intriguing.'

'Maybe. The police don't think Will's death was suspicious but his flatmate did. Will was phobic about needles, smoked his heroin, but the overdose that killed him was injected.'

She'd been listening with mock enthusiasm but her face became serious now, realizing the kind of story she was being told. She put her wine glass down and said, 'Did you speak to the police?' He nodded. 'And what did they say?'

'They said they'd looked at all the options but there was nothing to indicate a struggle, nothing to suggest it wasn't self-administered.'

'So the flatmate's paranoid.'

The conclusion grated a little, Alex conscious that the same could probably be said of him, with plenty of justification too.

'Maybe. I thought the same. But I was outside the church earlier and a few of Rob's colleagues were talking about him. Apparently his death doesn't add up either.' She looked cynical. 'Like I said, I'm just putting it before you. Apparently Rob was tipped off that there was something interesting at this farm. He went out there and just after he arrived the Americans decided to bomb it.'

'He was killed by our own side?'

'Friendly fire.'

'Jesus.' She looked upset by the thought of it. 'Still, don't you think it's just journalists' talk? They love a good conspiracy theory, and, let's be honest, it seems like a pretty random and over-the-top way of killing someone.'

'I agree.'

'And a motive. Why would someone kill Rob?' The working of her thoughts became briefly visible, her eyes darting about as she put together everything he'd told her, coming to the only possible conclusion. 'You're not serious?'

'Like I said, I'm just putting it before you like it is.'

She looked around, and lowered her voice as she said, 'No one knew about it. And even if they did, why would they wait ten years? Jesus, why would they do it at all? No. No, Alex, it's like the stuff of bad fiction.'

'Well, it's about to get worse. I'm not nailing my colours to the mast on this, just making the case that's there.'

'Yeah, so you keep saying.' She was irritated, as if she didn't want this to be about any more than the sad but accidental death of a friend, as if she didn't even want to be reminded of that night, her flight to denial total and unyielding.

'If by some extraordinary fluke, someone who wanted

revenge had found out about it they'd have gone to the police. Even if they'd wanted a more biblical revenge, I don't think they'd have gone to such extreme lengths to make the deaths look accidental. That would only be really crucial if you couldn't afford to have anyone linking the deaths and the people concerned.'

She stared at him, her eyes revealing again the swift calculation that was going on behind them. Finally she said, 'I see; a precaution that would of course be required by one of us though. And how fortunate that you have a convenient scapegoat for your theory.'

'What do you mean?'

'I mean Matt. Clearly you're ruling yourself out, and if you suspected me I don't think we'd be having this conversation.' Her voice became more sarcastic as she said, 'That leaves Matt, luckily the right nationality to have engineered Rob's death. And we all know the kind of background Matt comes from, don't we? It even explains the ten years. No doubt he's about to make a run for the Presidency and wants to eliminate any problematic hangovers from his wild student days. Seriously, Alex, when you write the book I promise I'll buy a copy, and I hope it has gold letters on the front because I love a really trashy read.'

'Like I said—'

She cut in angrily. 'No, fuck what you said! Have you completely forgotten the kind of person Matt MacAndrew was? Did you ever know him? I have no idea how to explain this, or even if there's anything to explain, but you should be ashamed of yourself for suggesting Matt would have anything to do with it.'

He didn't respond at first, surprised by the strength of her feelings. It seemed unlikely that Matt was behind it, that was true, but the whole thing was unlikely and yet two people were already dead. She looked furious though, perhaps part of the same denial, wanting to believe in some idealized airbrushed memory of the past.

He smiled and said, 'You're smarter than I remember.'

She smiled back, struggling momentarily to regain her angry composure. 'You're certainly a lot more fucking flaky than I remember.'

'Which proves the point that we've all changed.'

She shook her head, saying, 'Nice try.'

'Okay, I'll admit, Matt probably isn't behind this, if there's anything to be behind. All I know is, two old friends have died in as many weeks and I'm casting round here, looking for explanations, and the last thing I need is to hear that you or Matt have been killed too. It's not a nice thought to suggest one of us might be responsible but I'd rather upset you with that thought and have you vigilant than have you walking around in happy ignorance of the danger.'

She smiled and put her hand on his where it lay on the table, an action that reminded him of the woman in the church, comforting the grief-stricken man.

'Let's not talk about it, okay?' He shrugged, deferring. She let go of his hand then and looked around, saying, 'Where's our food?'

He looked around too but felt unsatisfied, annoyed with himself for not making a convincing case. She was probably right, about Matt in particular, but 'probably' wasn't much of an assurance. And for all the quickness of her thinking, she was no more clear about this than he was.

He was paranoid perhaps, hemmed in by his own guilt and remorse, but she was like someone in complete denial, not wanting to be reminded of the truth they shared. What had happened to them ten years before was as much in the realm of bad fiction as what was happening now, but it had happened all the same.

In the real world the worst plots imaginable forced their way into people's ordered lives. Five kids driving home from a party have a girl throw herself in front of their car. An addict gets murdered with his own drug of escape. A reporter follows a false lead and gets blown straight into the obituary columns. The real world *was* bad fiction.

Even so, they talked about other things as they ate, the relationships that had come and gone, their careers, families. Natalie was interested in his research but ignored all the obvious cues about his own sleep problems, displaying a skilful determination not to be led back into parts of the past she didn't want to revisit.

Only as they sat afterwards did Alex manage to drag the conversation back to where he felt he needed it to be.

'Have you kept in touch with Matt at all since college?'

She shook her head, regretful. 'I probably wouldn't have kept in touch with anyone. You know, after we split up' – she laughed to herself – 'after you let me go, I kind of didn't want to hear reports of how you were doing, and they were all your friends more than they were mine.'

'No they weren't. We were all equals.'

She smiled, disagreeing but not bothering to argue the point, and said, 'Well, the bottom line is, I was hurt, and like a wounded animal does, I hid myself away, in my work as it happens. Then Rob kind of tracked me down. We used to speak on the phone, which was funny because I never actually liked Rob that much back in college.'

'You're kidding?' It had never occurred to Alex that any of them had disliked each other.

'No, and we didn't speak often on the phone, but he became a much nicer person after we graduated, and I got to liking him a lot.' She paused and Alex wasn't sure if she was upset about Rob or thinking about what she wanted to say next. Maybe it was a bit of both. 'I always felt sorry for Will. Can't say I knew him well considering we were friends for three years, but I felt sorry for him. I thought Matt was great, and I have to say I regret that I didn't keep in touch with him. Which leaves you, and of course, I was in love with you. I tried so hard not to show how desperate I was for you to come to London with me, but even while you were telling me things were fine, it was like you were closing down on me.'

None of them had been good friends to each other, not the way they should have been, but Alex felt increasingly like he was the one who'd disappointed most, not just Natalie but all of them. 'I'm sorry,' he said, 'I never realized.'

'Something which was all too apparent at the time. I hope she was worth it.'

He was confused for a second, uncomfortable, but realized what she was saying then. 'Nat, there was no one else. I was stupid, that's all. I didn't even realize I was letting you go; it just happened. But there was no one else, believe me.'

She smiled a little and said, 'That might have been some consolation if you'd told me ten years ago. Still, it was probably for the best. I mean, really, what are the chances it would have survived anyway? Adult life and all that?'

She was dismissing it but the realization of the kind of friend and boyfriend he'd been was embedding itself now. Maybe if he'd made more effort then, the present situation would never have arisen. He couldn't help but think he'd played the biggest part in allowing them all to become estranged the way they had.

'I'm going to America,' said Alex, saying the thought as it occurred to him, realizing only afterwards that it made him look cold, oblivious to what she'd been saying. 'Sorry, I didn't mean to change the subject. You're right. If circumstances had been different I'd have come with you and I regret that things weren't different, but maybe it wouldn't have lasted anyway.'

She gave a cursory nod, distracted, and said, 'What do you mean, you're going to America? You mean, to work?'

'No, I mean I'm going to America this week, or as soon as I can arrange it. I want to see Matt, I want to speak to him for myself.'

'You could telephone him,' she said, her tone suggesting that a trip out there seemed like an overreaction.

'No, I want to speak to him in person. I want to see for myself, to believe for myself, that he isn't behind this. And I just want to talk to him about that night, about everything, things I should have told him ten years ago.'

She looked troubled by what he was saying, or confused perhaps, and said then, 'What are you talking about? Things you should have told him ten years ago – what things?'

'I just want to talk to him,' he said, sidestepping the question.

She still looked uncomfortable and said, 'I'm worried about this, Alex. I mean, if Matt *is* behind Rob's death, and I still think that's ridiculous, but if he is behind it you'd have to be crazy to waltz right into his own backyard like that.'

She was right about the last part but, unlike her, Alex was beginning to see the possibility of Matt being involved in the deaths as scarily credible, not the Matt they'd known but the one who'd developed over the last ten years, driven by ambition perhaps, or family expectation. That was why he wanted to go, to stare him in the face and see for himself.

'I agree, it's crazy, but think about it: if Matt's behind these deaths then he probably intends to kill us anyway. I'm sure he'll find that easier at a distance than he would face to face.'

'And if he isn't?'

'Then I get to see him and talk.' He smiled at her and said, 'Nat, I know you think I'm paranoid, but I need to do this, and I want you to do something for me.'

'What?'

'Go away for a week or so, go somewhere no one knows, lie low, just until I get back.' She shook her head and sighed. 'I'm serious, Nat. Look, you can't deny two of our former friends have died. Surely you can at least accept the possibility that there might be more to those deaths than meets the eye.'

'In theory,' she said, still grudging him the ground.

'Fine – in theory. So just go away until I find out.' He could see she'd take more convincing than that, and as a fallback position he said, 'At the very least, please, be more vigilant, a lot more, just for the next couple of weeks.'

She smiled, perhaps seeing beyond his edginess to the fact that he was concerned for her safety.

'Okay,' she said, 'I'll be more vigilant. And look, I'm due some time off, so I'll consider that too.' He smiled and she added, 'I said I'll consider it, that's all. And as it happens, I do think you're paranoid and I want you to promise me something in return. When you finally accept that no one is trying to kill us, I want you to get help.'

He laughed, saying, 'Jesus, I think I have a right to be a little paranoid in the light of what's happened these past few weeks. I'd hardly say it was a case for medical intervention. All I want is for you to be careful until I get back.'

'If you get back,' she said, smiling, showing that she still didn't take his conspiracy theory seriously. 'Anyway, how will you find him? Do you know where he's living now?'

'No, but I know where his family lives. I'll start there and see how it goes.'

She nodded and then looked absentmindedly at her watch, caught out by the time she saw there. 'Fuck, I should go.'

She looked for the waiter and Alex said, 'Leave it. I'll get this.'

'Do you mind? Thanks.' She got up and kissed him hastily on the cheek, then took a piece of paper from her bag and wrote her number on it. 'Seriously, Alex, call me when you get back. We'll do this again, without the doom and gloom next time.'

He said something but she was already walking away, her mind focused on work again, as if she'd brought the shutters down on the past, an abrupt closure. She'd been convinced that he was in need of help and yet as he thought about her afterwards, he couldn't help but think that she was the one who'd changed.

There was a subtle difference in the person he'd just been talking to, like a small but vital circuit had failed somewhere, the damage impacting on everything she said, on her feelings, on who she was. It was still the same Natalie but something inside her had died, a loss to which she was herself apparently oblivious.

He couldn't pin it down because the change was so slight, but it was there. The Natalie he'd known ten years ago would have been stopped in her tracks by the news of Will's death. This Natalie had stopped in her tracks too but he wasn't sure if she'd done it because it had seemed the right thing to do, or even simply because they'd reached the restaurant.

He paid the bill and walked along the street to the tube

station, making his way through the mix of business people and foreign tourists, standing near the edge of the platform with people gradually building behind him, some Italian girls the only people talking.

A train seemed to approach but the noise subsided again, the tunnel mouth remaining black and empty. He heard someone say, 'Alex,' and turned to look behind him. No one was looking at him, no one he recognized either. He faced forward and a few seconds later he heard it again, a loud whisper right behind him, 'Alex!'

He spun around, staring accusingly at the other people there, most of them averting their gazes from him. He was embarrassed, realizing he'd imagined it. He turned back but looked down at the track in front of him and got a sudden violent feeling that he was about to be pushed. It gave him the shakes, the fear total and instant, for all his attempts to rationalize.

He heard the rushing wind sound of the train coming and saw it emerge from the tunnel. People began to move around him, a volatile flux of bodies, and there was the track looming up below him, the fierce wheels of the train approaching.

He panicked, turned and pushed back quickly, back towards the curved wall with its glazed bricks and posters, pushing past the people in his way. He was sweating, eyes darting around the faces of the other passengers, some of them staring at him now but looking away quickly as he made eye contact.

They thought he was acting strangely perhaps, drunk or crazy or on drugs. And he was acting strangely; Alex himself was able to maintain enough distance to see that. Standing on the edge of that platform though, nothing else had been more real than the feeling that he was about to be pushed.

It would have been convenient too, if someone was trying to kill them all. A death on the tube – suicide or accidental, no one would have thought twice. Even if people had asked questions, what would they have been told? That he'd been distressed at the death of a friend, had fainted on hearing the news, had been acting out of character.

He pushed on to the train once it had stopped and stood with his back to the carriage partition, still studying the other people, becoming more comfortable only as the faces changed station by station, a foreign family with small children the only people left who'd boarded with him.

And as he began to relax the pendulum swung back in the other direction and he was embarrassed, angry with himself for losing his cool like that. It made him more determined, too, that he'd go to America and see Matt, because he couldn't go on like this, his mind slipping into a surreal struggle with itself.

He needed to speak to Matt, to find out one way or another whether he was involved in these deaths, and he needed to speak to him about that night ten years ago, about the things he knew, the truth. Whoever Matt had become, he still needed to speak to him, to put things right, or at least those few things that could still be put to rights.

It had been overcast in the morning but the sky had cleared now and as he walked into the long street where Rob had lived the sun was shining as brightly as it had a couple of weeks before. The white houses looked fresh and bright, the small trees that lined the road looking like they were about to bud.

It was cold though and he kept his overcoat on and walked quickly. He rang the bell a couple of times when he got there but got no response, the house giving out no sound. The cremation was for family only but he'd heard people talking about some sort of reception so maybe Rebecca had gone there.

He checked his watch and then sat down on the step, loosening the black tie before taking it off altogether and putting it in his overcoat pocket. He kept his coat huddled around him but the sun was warm on his face and time turned fluid as he sat there, marked only by the occasional car or pedestrian passing on the quiet street.

He wasn't looking out for her but turned at the sound of heels clacking steadily up the street. It was Rebecca, wearing a short black skirt and jacket but with a beige raincoat over the top, still giving the impression somehow that she wasn't used to dressing formally.

He guessed she'd seen him but she didn't look in his direction, even though he kept his eyes fixed on her as she approached. She kept looking ahead, dignified, composed, her features fixed. She was almost at the house but still didn't look, and then, as if she hadn't seen him, she walked past and continued along the street.

He turned, puzzled, and looked at the house number, hearing the footsteps come to a stop then. When he turned back she was standing a few yards away smiling at him.

'Have you seen *The Third Man*?'

'No.'

She threw her arms up and said, 'So much for that. I was re-enacting the final scene. Alex, you must have seen it! Orson Welles?'

He shook his head as she walked back towards him. 'Sorry. Am I Orson Welles?'

She was standing over him now, the smile still there but fading as she said, 'Joseph Cotten. Orson Welles is dead. I was his girlfriend.' Alex stood up and she regrouped the smile before saying, 'Cup of tea?'

'Sure.'

She opened the door and let him in, pointing towards the kitchen. He walked through, glad that she was in good enough spirits, but hovered for a while then, wondering why she hadn't followed him in. Finally he stepped back into the hall and looked towards the door.

She'd got no further than putting the lock on behind her, had slid down the wall where she was crouched now, her head buried in her arms, weeping silently, only the movement of her shoulders giving her away. His heart sank. He thought this was why he'd come, to comfort her, and yet now he was here facing it, he didn't know what to do or what he had to offer.

He walked along the hall and stood above her, made to put his hand on her shoulder but stopped, feeling hopelessly, ridiculously English. He sank down on to his knees instead and put his hand on hers, the small reassuring gesture he'd already seen twice today.

She looked up, her face more composed than he'd expected but run with tears. She wiped her eyes with her free hand and said, 'This is so bloody stupid. I hardly knew him.' This was how people were; they cried for the people they'd lost.

'I don't think it's stupid at all.'

'I could have really fallen for him,' she said, her face disfiguring with emotion, a fresh pulse of tears running down her cheeks.

'Come on,' he said, helping her up, 'let's have that cup of tea.'

He made the tea, guided through the process with instructional asides from her as she talked, where the cups were, the tea bags. There'd been a reception at a hotel, Rebecca talking about the people who were there before asking him where he'd gone after the service.

'I went to lunch.'

'With that girl you were talking to?'

He liked that she'd seen him, that he hadn't been completely invisible.

'Natalie, yeah. She was at college with us.' He put the cups of tea on the table in front of her and sat down, the place where Rob had sat a couple of weeks before, not that it mattered or was significant.

'So that's who she was – your ex?' He nodded. 'She looked really devastated during the service.' He was surprised, thinking she'd been pretty composed afterwards. She'd been a little erratic too though, like someone only just holding it together, the same person who he felt was still too deeply in denial about the past to cope particularly well with fresh traumas. Rebecca sipped at her tea and said, 'You're not very emotional yourself, are you, Alex?'

'How do you mean?'

'I watched you at the funeral. I was pretty impressed at first but, I don't know, it was almost like you didn't feel anything at all.' He nodded thoughtfully, and a moment later she said, 'Oh, Jesus, that sounded terrible. Sorry, I didn't mean to . . .'

'No, you're right, it's what I was thinking myself, that I wasn't sure if I felt anything at all. The guy next to me was crying and I couldn't, just, I don't know. I couldn't understand what he was feeling that would make him cry like that. I want to feel like that, but I can't.'

'You're not missing much. I suppose it didn't help either, that the two of you had only just met up again.'

'No,' he said, refusing her excuses. 'It makes me angry that we wasted ten years. But nothing had changed, you know. I loved him, I really did. Nat was my girlfriend. Will, he was a good friend, but he was almost like the stray we took in. Rob and Matt and me, I think we had something pretty special.'

She smiled, looking warmed by the thought, but said then, 'So what happened?'

'Life happened. Life and death, and before you know it you're sitting at a funeral wondering why you're not upset.' It wasn't much of an explanation, but then there weren't many adequate explanations for what had happened to their friendship.

She smiled, rubbing his arm as she said, 'You shouldn't worry about it too much. Jesus, you're probably in shock. I could tell the way you and Rob felt about each other. He was so bloody excited that you were coming down. Seriously, I might as well have been at uni with you – I know everything that happened.'

He laughed, a quiet internal voice still correcting her, that she didn't know everything. They talked about college though, about Rob, satisfying a need they both had to recall him and then it was time for him to leave.

She walked out with him and stood on the step, the sky still blue but edging darker, the sun lost somewhere over the rooftops.

'Thanks for coming round.'

'I wanted to come.'

She kissed him on the cheek and said, 'Well, if you're ever in town, you know where I am.' He nodded and there was a moment of silence; they both knew they'd probably never meet again. Alex couldn't even keep the people in his life who were meant to be there, always pushing them away despite himself. She looked up the street and said, 'You taking the tube?'

He looked at his watch. 'No, I'll probably flag a taxi. There's a train in half an hour so I'll try to make that.'

'Okay, take care, Alex.'

'You too.' He walked down the steps but turned then, suddenly acutely aware that he knew almost nothing about her. She looked more informal now, still in the dark suit but physically relaxed, an easy attractiveness. 'What do you do, Rebecca? I can't believe I haven't even asked.'

'I'm a doctor.'

'Oh.'

She acknowledged his surprise by laughing, saying, 'What, you assumed I probably had some chick job? Clothes shop attendant, publicist, something like that?'

'Red-handed,' he said, adding, 'My brother's a doctor, in Edinburgh.'

'I know. I thought you were, too.'

'Except I don't make people better.'

'You help them sleep. I'd say that was making them better.'

'I don't do that any more. It's not even why I went into this field.'

She smiled. 'So why did you?'

'I don't know. Maybe it's just where I want to be.'

He smiled and walked away along the street, thinking over what he'd just said. He'd never put it like that before. He'd always known that his interest in his subject had been linked to the incidents he suffered himself. He'd realized too that his studies could easily be playing a part in perpetuating the attacks.

It had never occurred to him though that a part of him might want the attacks to continue. It seemed an extraordinary idea even now, that he could be compelled to something that disturbed him so much, that reduced him to living life as if within a photographic negative.

Yet now that he'd thought of it, the concept smacked of truth and he was amazed that he'd been blind to it for so long. He wondered, too, whether Ruth had considered the possibility. Alex had the excuse of being too deeply involved to see the obvious but Ruth had to have seen it.

It was probably one of the things she'd always wanted to ask him, and if she'd asked him in the past he would have denied it. Maybe he still would now, not through ignorance but fear, because it was something to face up to, the idea that he might actually want Emily Barratt to come to him in his sleep, and that for all his science, some deeply buried part of his psyche wanted to believe she was real.

11

The breath burst back into his lungs. He let out an involuntary cry and sprang from the bed, shaking, fumbling for the light switch, scanning the room quickly. He looked at the video cameras. He was awake now, that was all that mattered. He breathed deeply and tried to concentrate but the air still seemed loaded with that sickly sweet smell.

She was there somewhere. He heard the creak of the stair and ran out on to the landing, hitting the light switch. The air below stirred and he followed it quickly, down to the hall, into the harsh light of the kitchen, realizing then what had happened, the trauma of the dream finally falling back into the depths.

He fell down on to one of the chairs, his heart sick with its own blood, his T-shirt cold and clammy against his back, exhaustion pulling him down. Rogue thoughts of her presence continued to fire but he was fully conscious now, able to reason against them and dismiss it. He drank some water and made his way back upstairs, his spine still shuddering as he moved through the rooms.

Back in the bedroom he picked up his watch and checked the time, still before three, and sank on to the bed, sitting there for a few minutes before accepting that he was too afraid to go back to sleep, that there was no point anyway when it left him like this.

Besides, his mind was fired up now, the presence of Emily Barratt opening the gates to all the other related ghosts, of Rob and Will and the impending confrontation with Matt, the ghost he'd become of himself. What good was there in trying to sleep?

He got dressed slowly, every movement an effort, got himself together and went out, the night cold and starlit, reviving him, a chill wind that made him pull his coat tight around him, digging his hands into the deep pockets. He walked, relishing the elements, the feeling of being alive out there.

He walked through the pedestrianized centre of town, no one about, no movement, and even on the other side of it there were only occasional cars passing, taxis or police cars looking for non-existent trouble. Friday or Saturday night there would have been a tension in the air, even at that time, but tonight the town was his own.

At first he didn't think he was heading anywhere in particular, just not towards the river, a place that always drew him but left him morose. He walked on steadily in the opposite direction, twenty minutes or so, and whether it had been chance or a subconscious impulse, he saw that he was only a short distance from the place where the accident had happened.

His adrenaline picked up with the thought of it. He'd never been there since, had never even driven down that road, and yet now he couldn't understand why. He wanted to see it again, thinking it would help him somehow to go there, part of the process of finally coming to terms with it and what it meant to him.

He turned left, walked a little further, then right, into the long tree-lined street of big houses that swept an arc through the southern suburbs of the town. The houses were Victorian, elegant relics of a lost middle class, most of them housing the student children of a new middle class now.

Here and there as he walked there were still lights on behind some of the overgrown hedges and shrubs that made up the front gardens, music playing faintly, the smell of food cooking in one house, bacon perhaps, and laughter too from the same place. It made him want to be inside with some of those people, to be one of them.

He pressed on though, alone, the wind blowing a chorus through the gardens, the bare branches of the trees forming dancing shadows where the streetlights caught them. About halfway along the street he stopped and walked out into the road. There was nothing to mark the place in his memory but he guessed this had to be about where it had happened.

He looked on, imagining the car stopped up ahead, the interior light on, passenger door open, a trail of exhaust drifting into the cold air. He thought of her too, lying on the tarmac, and somewhere along here was the point from which she'd darted out in front of them.

He moved back to the edge of the road now and tried to imagine how they hadn't seen her. There were a few cars parked on the street tonight whereas there hadn't been ten years before. The trees were big though, forming a complex backdrop of shadows with the overgrown gardens that lay just behind them.

And the truth was, Matt's reactions had undoubtedly been slower than they should have been, what with the drinks he'd had, the mood in the car, the quietness of the early hours. Even if he'd been concentrating fully she could still have surprised him from those shadows. She'd come at them quickly too, he remembered that, or at least, that's how it had seemed.

He looked at the houses again, wondering whether she'd come out of one of them. Unlike Will, he'd always tried to avoid the press coverage and the speculation, but he'd heard enough to know that it had been a mystery what she'd been doing there. None of her friends had known of anyone she might have visited in the street.

That meant nothing though. The whole nature of student society was meeting new people, going to new places. She could easily have met someone and visited them without telling her friends. What had always troubled Alex was that she'd been alone, that her friends hadn't been with her, that whoever she'd been with had seen fit to let her walk home alone.

Will had been obsessed with the idea that she'd been running away from someone, that the five of them had simply provided the last act of an evening that had already been a nightmare for her. The truth was probably more mundane, that her judgement had been as subtly skewed by alcohol as theirs had.

He looked around, the wild dark feel of the street. Possibly she'd simply been walking along it and, spooked, had started to run, chased by shadows into the road. There was an irony there if that was the truth, Alex himself chased by the same shadows ever since, maybe the others too.

He heard a car engine and turned. A large black car came slowly along the street, not a student car. He couldn't see into it but the car slowed further as it reached him, as if the driver wanted to see who was there by the edge of the road. Alex stared back, holding his nerve, and the car accelerated again.

For a moment he imagined the driver being the person who'd found her that night, someone equally haunted, drawn back to the same location in the hope of making sense of it. It had never occurred to him before, that somewhere out there was the person who'd found her, another curse they'd handed down.

He started to walk back, following the fading tail lights of the car. He didn't really want to go back to the house but there was nothing else to see here and no further to walk without looking suspicious. Maybe even here he looked suspicious, the reason the car had slowed.

He was almost back to the centre of town when he saw a couple of students on the road ahead and then a taxi pulling up for them. He didn't want to go back to the house and, seizing the opportunity, he ran a little to get there before they got into the cab. The two young guys looked nervous at first that someone was running towards them, then quietly hostile.

He was out of breath but smiled as he got there, saying, 'Are you on your way to campus?'

They were reluctant to answer but the taxi driver looked out of the window, assuming perhaps that Alex was talking to him, and said, 'That's right, campus, name of Barnetson.'

Alex smiled again, more broadly now, realizing how these two kids really didn't want to share their taxi; it reminded him of the way he and the others had been as students.

'Don't mind if I share your cab, do you? I'll get the fare.'

They looked at each other, their minds too slow in coming up with an excuse or answer. Alex didn't wait anyway, getting in the front next to the driver.

'Whereabouts?'

Alex looked at him and said, 'It's their cab. I want the Psychology Department but I'll walk from wherever they're going.'

The driver looked in the rear-view and one of them said quietly, 'Balmer College, please.'

The driver nodded and pulled away.

Alex turned slightly in his seat and said, 'That used to be my college.' They nodded, unfriendly, not saying anything. He smiled anyway, exhilarated for some reason, a sense that he was escaping, doing something.

When they got to Balmer the two students offered to pay their share but Alex insisted and they thanked him curtly before getting out and disappearing quickly into the college, concerned perhaps that he'd try to tag along. He paid and walked in the other direction, cutting between buildings to the Psychology Department.

Ruth looked to the door as he swiped his card, seeing him through the glass. She smiled but looked puzzled.

'Couldn't sleep,' he said, as he walked in.

'Did you have an episode? You look like you did.'

'Why, how do I look?'

'Like you had an episode,' she said, smiling.

He shrugged his shoulders and said, 'It wasn't anything to speak of. I just didn't feel much like sleeping afterwards. I went out for a walk and then I decided to come and see what you were up to.'

She pointed at the monitoring equipment and said, 'Just one volunteer, second time he's been in for me. He wakes of his own accord at the end of each REM, has a full recollection of his dreams, which are nearly always lucid.'

'And you've only had him in here twice?'

She nodded regretfully, acknowledging that the volunteer in there was the kind of opportunity that came along once in a lifetime.

'Not for want of trying. Unlike us, he seems to have a pretty successful social life.'

Alex took his coat off, caught up in a resurgence of enthusiasm for his subject.

'Have you interviewed him at any length yet?' She nodded. 'He hasn't trained himself to wake? Doesn't keep a dream diary?'

'No. In fact, until he came in here last time he wasn't aware that it was unusual.'

'Lucky him. You mind if I look at your notes?'

'Of course not.' He sat down and looked over Ruth's notes but now that he was sitting he felt tired again and couldn't concentrate on the words in front of him. He put on an act of studying them but he could feel the world slipping in and out of focus and when Ruth spoke her voice had the echoing acoustics of the slide into sleep.

'Alex, you look really tired.'

He sat upright with a jolt and looked at her, smiling, about to deny it but conscious of how he must have looked, his eyes heavy, a drunk's demeanour.

'I suppose I must be.' He sighed heavily with the thought of going back home.

Ruth could obviously see his reluctance, perhaps even sensing what was behind it, and said, 'Why don't you crash here for a couple of hours? It's probably all you need, a couple of hours.'

He looked at the door to the bedrooms and said, 'You've been wanting to get me into bed for ages.'

She laughed and said, 'It's what I dream about, Dr Stratton, it really is. But seriously, no wires. Just crash for a couple of hours.'

'Will you wake me?' She nodded and he got up smiling and walked through, struggling against tiredness to take some of his clothes off before crashing on to the bed.

He was too tired even to worry about having another attack, but he felt secure there, a place he'd made his own, more than he had his own house. That was a place he'd ceded to Emily Barratt, as though she'd wandered the town until she'd found him and then claimed it for herself.

The taxi journey and the surly students replayed as he drifted into sleep, and Ruth's voice, like it often did. No dreams followed that he could recall but he didn't seem to sleep for long. He checked his watch when he woke: just after seven. He got up and went to the bathroom, then went back through to Ruth.

She wasn't there. He guessed she was in with her volunteer so he went through and put the kettle on for coffee. When he came back she was there, going over her notes. She looked tired herself now, blood-drained, like the cold of early morning was beginning to get to her.

She looked up and smiled, relieved to have some company perhaps, and said, 'Did anything cross your mind?'

He smiled too, the standard sleep researcher's question to the woken volunteer. 'I haven't been much good to you, have I, Ruth?'

'Are you kidding?' She looked genuinely amazed. 'You've been great. You've always been there when I needed help, you've let me do my own thing when I haven't. What else could you have done?'

'True, I suppose. I just feel I could have been more supportive.'

'Alex, you haven't slept long enough. Seriously, studying with you has been one of the best opportunities of my life.'

He raised his eyebrows, a self-deprecating smile, saying, 'I've made coffee. Do you want one?'

'Yes, please.' Before he could walk away though, she said, 'You know, I get the impression you've kind of lost faith in what you do over the last year, maybe even lost interest, but you shouldn't downplay the stuff you've done in the past, groundbreaking stuff, and it doesn't matter what your reason for doing it was. You did it, that's all that matters.'

He nodded a little and said, 'Thanks, I appreciate that, and I know.' He went out and got the coffee.

She was right of course, not so much about his contribution but about losing faith, losing interest, losing his way. He'd taken a sabbatical to work on his new book and yet hadn't really worked at all in three months, wasting the days, sitting at his desk each night shuffling papers, rearranging his notes, pretending to work but only biding time, waiting for what was to come.

When he came back from America he'd have to do something about that. It seemed possible too, because in some stubborn part of his mind he'd decided that going to America and seeing Matt was the first step in freeing himself. There was no great logic in it but he held fast to the thought.

He was still conscious of the other possible outcome though, and as he sat with Ruth making small talk over the coffee he was thinking about it. When she finally mentioned the impending trip to America he answered briefly and then said, 'I know this is silly, but say my plane were to crash, I'd like to believe that you might stay on here. I don't know, maybe even expand it, turn it into a real unit.'

'Don't worry, if your plane crashes, I'll stay.' She smiled and said, 'You never know, I might even stay if your plane doesn't crash.'

He gave her a concerned look, lifted his hand and said, 'How many fingers am I holding up?' She laughed, a sleepy laugh that he found warming somehow. He thought over what had been preoccupying him the last couple of days and decided it was perhaps finally the time to ask her about it.

He said, 'Tell me something, Ruth, has it ever occurred to you that I might not actually want my attacks to cease?'

She looked almost offended, an injured look in her eyes as she said, 'Of course it has.'

'So why have you never said anything?'

'How would you have reacted?' He didn't answer and she said, 'Exactly. Anyway, teasing aside, I've never wanted to push you into talking about it. If you want to tell me you will. I'd never want to force a decision that personal on to someone.'

He nodded. 'If ever I tell anyone, it'll be you.' She smiled, not believing him. 'So go on, what other suspicions have you never shared with me?'

'You won't be offended?'

'Since when has that worried you?'

She shrugged and said, 'Okay. I think you know who she is. I think it's someone you know, or knew, maybe some ex-girlfriend who died. And I think you know why you have the attacks, that you could stop them but that, like you said, you don't want them to stop. Perhaps because they keep her alive in your head.'

He'd had to put on a poker face at first as he'd listened to her but he'd relaxed more as she'd talked on, and now he smiled and said, 'Not bad, but, touch wood, I've never had a girlfriend die on me. And maybe I have been ambivalent about stopping the attacks, but, trust me, I'm in the process of stopping them now.'

He felt that was true, that these two strands back to the past had become entwined and that he could bring a halt to both of them simultaneously, the process starting with the visit to Matt. If Matt really was behind the deaths of Will and Rob, he didn't know whether the things he had to say would be enough.

He'd go anyway though, because the process of freeing himself would begin with Matt too. He'd talk to him, finally tell him the truth of what had happened that night. If Matt had changed beyond recognition it was probably information that would mean nothing to him, but that wouldn't matter, because it wasn't only Matt's forgiveness he was after, it was his own.

12

He didn't sleep on the plane. He was tired but he didn't sleep, uneasy about the thought of having an attack in front of other people. It wouldn't matter how much he tried to dismiss it, the attendants would have him marked as someone to keep their eye on, other passengers staring at him like he was disturbed.

Instead he thought feverishly over the things he'd need to do, mental checklists too of the things he'd already done, thinking over other contingencies, anything to keep his mind falsely alert. He'd already thought through these things a hundred times but he didn't want to sleep.

He'd considered writing something out before leaving, handing it to his solicitor with instructions that it be published if he died in mysterious circumstances. He hadn't though, the whole thing finally seeming too fanciful, too absurd. And anyway, what was mysterious? Rob's death? Will's?

In the end all he did was put his notes for his book in some kind of order and telephone Natalie. He got her answering machine, an indication, he hoped, that she'd taken his advice and gone to ground. He left a message anyway, saying he'd get in touch as soon as he got back.

By the time the flight arrived he was beginning to struggle with the tiredness, convincing himself that it might even be more than tiredness. He was burning up as he made his slow progress from plane to taxi, feeling light-headed, reaching out to steady himself every time he had to stand still.

The taxi driver was foreign, East European perhaps, and when Alex gave him the address he looked at him as if he wasn't making sense. He drove off anyway and Alex relaxed a little, swimming in and out of hallucinations, seeing the cabin of the plane through the taxi windows, the attendants walking around serving dinner.

He lurched back into consciousness a few times but had little idea where he was, little awareness of their progress into the city, and when the taxi driver spoke to him he was startled and confused.

They were stopped in traffic, the taxi driver looking around at him, saying, 'Which way?'

Alex looked out of the window, unsure at first where they were. 'We're in Manhattan,' he said.

The driver looked at him like he was crazy and said, 'Yeah, Manhattan. Which way?' His accent was heavy but already developing New York edges.

Alex reached into his pocket and gave him the piece of paper with Kate's address on it.

The taxi driver shrugged and said again, 'Which way?' A horn beeped behind them and he drove, muttering to himself.

'I don't know,' said Alex. 'Near Columbia University?' He was guessing. He wouldn't have been able to direct the guy to Kate's old apartment but he'd never even been to this one, and as the confusion ebbed away he was amused that he'd picked a comedian's idea of a New York cab driver.

He felt livelier now, like he'd stepped through the tiredness, looking out at the bustling streets, making suggestions, none of which the driver seemed to understand or find helpful. The driver was talking to himself now anyway, working his way through the puzzle in his own language, looking up at every street sign.

When they finally got there Alex gave him a hefty tip, feeling guilty for some reason because he hadn't known the way. The driver seemed dismissive though, like it was the least he'd expected, acknowledging the fact that Alex had been a difficult customer.

It tickled him, a good story to tell Kate, break the ice. He climbed the steps and rang the bell, using the doorway as best he could to shelter from the fierce wind. She answered, excited, buzzing him up. Once inside the lobby he composed himself for a second, taking in how cold he'd got in the couple of minutes he'd been outside.

He took the lift up then, and walked along, counting off the door numbers. He reached hers but almost before he'd taken in the correct number the door flew open and she was standing facing him with a broad smile.

She was beautiful, more than he remembered, and even with the loose sweater there was an inviting warmth in the look of her body. Natalie had seemed attractive at Rob's funeral but he hadn't been attracted to her. Kate left him speechless though, an amnesiac suddenly remembering what his life had been.

He smiled but her own smile began to drop. Her eyes had been bright when she'd opened the door but looked sorrowful now, filling with tears. She started to cry and he dropped his bags and put his arms out to her.

'It can't be that bad to see me,' he said as she cried into his shoulder.

She laughed a little and pulled back, her face messed up with tears. Looking at him again brought on a fresh wave and her words were distorted as she said, 'You look terrible.'

'Thanks, it was a long flight.' She pointed at the bruise on his temple. 'Long and violent.' She laughed again and he took out a handkerchief and started to dry her tears with it. 'I'm really tired, that's all. The bruise is from a fall the other week. Jesus, I didn't think I looked that bad.'

She held him again, the softness of her body inviting as a bed, like a remedy for the sleep that had failed him more and more frequently over these last couple of years.

'I've missed you,' she said.

'Me too.' She eased away, closing the door.

She made a determined effort now to pull herself together and, gesturing to the room, she said, 'What do you think?'

He looked around and said, 'Nice. It reminds me of the other place.'

'The other place was a dump.' She was becoming more relaxed, getting comfortable with the change in the way he looked.

Alex was still rattled by the way she'd reacted but made an effort not to let it show. 'I don't remember it. Except the furniture, and that's the same.'

She smiled like he was teasing, though he really couldn't remember the old place looking any different, and then she seemed to spill over with things to say, offering him a seat, asking him if he wanted a drink, if he was hungry, whether he wanted to sleep now or hold off for a while.

'Actually, why don't you open some wine and I'll take a shower?'

'Good,' she said, relieved that he'd come to a decision.

He felt better when he came out of the shower, temporarily refreshed, awake. Kate was only just pouring the wine.

'I thought we'd order something in,' she said. 'I'd intended to take you out but I thought this might be nicer.'

'Embarrassed to be seen out with me, huh?'

'Well, it is a very style-conscious city.' He smiled, sitting on the sofa, taking the wine she offered. 'I just thought you looked so wrecked, and it hadn't occurred to me you'd be tired from the flight. We can go out tomorrow night, if you're here. Or the next night. Where is it you're going?'

'Garrington. I think it's essentially one of these little commuter towns. I'll go up tomorrow, stay the night. You must remember me talking about Matt, the American who was at college with us?'

'Of course, yes!' The whole trip appeared to make sense to her now, which was more than it did to him. 'So he's been in touch with you?'

'Not quite. He doesn't know I'm coming. In fact, I don't even know that he still lives there.'

Her face took on a look of confusion, an accurate enough reflection of Alex's own muddled thinking. She smiled and said, 'Let me get this right. You're visiting the parental home of someone you haven't seen for ten years in the hope that he still lives there or happens to be visiting?'

He wasn't sure how to answer. He didn't really expect to find Matt still living there. Matt was probably in New York or Washington, but Alex felt that by visiting his parents first he'd gain some advantage. He didn't like to admit it but, in truth, he was already treating Matt like an adversary, approaching him with as much caution as possible.

'I agree, it sounds crazy if you put it like that. He probably lives here in the city now, and, I know, I could have found that out by phoning. I didn't want to speak to him on the phone though.' She still looked bemused so he added, 'Two of our friends from college have died in the last few weeks. And I know we hadn't really kept in touch but we were pretty close back then; that's kind of been brought home to me in the last week or two. So I wanted to tell him in person.'

'How awful,' she said. 'Is it anyone I know about?'

'Remember the guy who used to write to me every now and then?'

'Wills?'

'Will, yeah. He died of a drug overdose. And Rob, the one who was a journalist, killed in Kosovo.'

'That's so sad.' He could see what she was thinking. She was imagining what it would be like to lose two friends like that. They were too young to have friends who'd died. She looked at him then and said, 'How have you been?'

'Okay, I suppose.' She nodded and left it at that. She was too smart not to have worked out that the absence of these close friends from his life was linked in some way to the attacks that disturbed his sleep. She'd never said anything about it though, steering clear of enquiries that would force the issue, respecting his need to keep it in the shadows. 'It has to be said, of course, that I came to see you too.'

'How convenient,' she said. He smiled. It hadn't been true but it felt like the truth now that he was here. It wasn't just that he'd forgotten how beautiful she was, more that he'd forgotten how good he felt when he was with her, settled, at peace.

She got up and said, 'I'll order some food. What do you feel like?'

'Up to you.'

'Vietnamese?'

'Fine. You choose.' She walked into the kitchen and he called after her, saying, 'My taxi driver had to ask me for directions.'

She laughed and shouted back, 'You're making that up!'

'I swear, I'm telling the truth. He asked me for directions, and of course I didn't have a clue. I'm here and I don't even know where I am.'

'We're just around the corner from my old place.'

'Easy for you to say.'

She appeared in the doorway, her voice quieter again as she said, 'No, I really do mean around the corner. Go over to the window and look to your left. If you turn right at the end of the street it's about twenty yards to my old building.'

'Oh.' He got up and went to the window as she walked back into the kitchen.

He opened it and leaned out, the sudden burst of cold air going through him as if his body lacked any resistance. The street was quiet below, a few people walking, lights on in most of the buildings across the way. The noise of traffic carried from each end.

He looked to the left, in the direction of the traffic. He had a vague recollection now of where he was, brought on more by the noise rather than any recognition of the buildings. And it still felt strange, a place he couldn't imagine Kate living.

She came back in and joined him at the window, huddling closer as she said, 'God, it's cold!' He didn't answer and she added, 'So you know where you are now?'

'Kind of. Not really. All the street numbers confuse me. I wish they all had names.'

'No, it makes sense after a while. You get used to it.'

They looked at some of the lit rooms opposite, silent films, and then Alex said, 'I haven't heard a siren yet.'

'Very funny.'

'No, I'm serious. I like to hear New York sirens. London sirens always sound seedy but in New York it's different. It's that whole Gershwin thing, you know.'

'Yeah, I know what you mean.' They fell back into silence.

169

He wanted to say something else at first but then felt comfortable just knowing she was there, the slight warmth of her body next to his. Finally she said, 'I can't get used to it.'

He was surprised by her words, by how quiet and lost they'd sounded. He turned to her and said, 'What do you mean?'

'I mean New York. It's great and everything, but I can't get used to it. Sometimes I just wish I was somewhere smaller, more intimate, less intimate, I don't know.'

'You've never said anything in your e-mails,' he said, still surprised by the sudden admission.

'I know. I've hardly dared accept it myself. Don't get me wrong, I love the teaching and I think I'll definitely stay out here. I'm just not much of a city girl.'

He nodded but didn't respond at first. He'd thought of her as thriving there and now here they were, two small figures shivering in a window in a city that was too big for them. He wanted to offer her solutions, thinking over the possibilities before realizing something else, something that had lain dormant for two years or more, that he wanted to be with her.

He wanted to say something but was nervous, afraid that he was just being drawn to the human warmth she offered, to the suddenly vivid memory of the years they'd lived together, years when the attacks had almost ceased. He was afraid of his motives, suspecting his own selfishness and confusion.

Yet what he was most nervous about was the risk of saying something and being rebuffed, Kate having to explain apologetically that her life had moved on, that she was seeing someone else.

It felt like it was worth the risk though, and trying to sound casual, he said, 'Maybe we should look for somewhere prestigious but provincial, somewhere with a great English Department and a sleep research programme.' She looked at him, trying to work out if he was being serious or teasing her with a picture of a future he'd never buy into. He felt encouraged by her expression, adding, 'Or just a good Psychology Department. I persuaded one university to let me set up a sleep research programme, and that was before I had a reputation.'

She stepped back in from the window, waiting for him to do the same before closing it.

'Alex, if I thought for one minute that you were serious.'

'I'm serious,' he said, becoming more enthused because she was cautious and hadn't laughed. 'I'm thinking on the move here, but I'm serious. I need to make a break with the past. And you know, maybe us being apart has been good, made us see what we had.'

'I always knew. You were the one who . . . I don't know. If I hadn't known better I'd have thought you were cheating on me. That's how it was, like you were with me physically but your mind was somewhere else.'

He could see how close he was; all she wanted was a commitment to the present, to what was before him.

'I know I was like that, and that's part of the reason I'm here, this trip to see Matt.' He walked over and sat back down, picking up his wine, taking another comforting sip, the soft blackcurrant taste filling his mouth. She sat down too and he said, 'I'm putting my life right. It sounds pompous but it's true. I'm putting everything right and I'm moving on.'

For a moment it looked like he'd lost her as she said, 'I don't suppose you want to enlighten me at all?'

He didn't answer the question but said, 'I should never have let you go, Kate. That's the only part that matters.'

She smiled and said, 'We're not sleeping together. If that's what this is all in aid of, you're wasting your time.'

He laughed at the accusation but looked around then and said, 'You have two bedrooms?'

'You can sleep in the bed with me but you know what I mean. You hurt me, Alex, not intentionally maybe, but you still hurt me and I don't intend to invest in this relationship again until I know you're serious.'

He nodded, happy that there was at least an opening, another reason to be determined about freeing himself. After a moment or two he said, 'Has there been anyone else?'

'I don't think that's any of your business, do you?' The indignation was light-hearted. 'There isn't anyone at the moment.' He nodded, disappointed that she didn't ask him the same question. He wasn't sure whether that was because she wasn't interested or just that she was pretty certain of the answer already. And yet he'd wanted her to ask, just to be able to tell her.

The food came and they talked about work as they ate, the familiar kind of catch-up conversation they'd had over dinner in the past. It felt like they were a couple again, as if in some small way they'd never stopped being a couple. And at the same time he couldn't keep his eyes off her, so much so that more than once she became self-conscious about it.

A couple of times over the evening he thought he'd probably be able to sway her on the matter of sleeping together. He didn't try though, caught up in the spirit of proving himself first. He was tired too, and still preoccupied. But he couldn't believe he'd forgotten how attractive she was, how much he wanted her.

When they went into bed she changed in the bathroom, coming out in a night-shirt, keeping up the pretence that they were friends rather than lovers. Perhaps it wasn't pretence though, and the intimacy they'd had was something they'd have to find all over again.

They shared the bed like friends too, Kate joking about why it had to be like this. It seemed strangely innocent, like some old screwball comedy, the two leads under no illusion as to where things were heading but still insisting on keeping their distance from each other.

Kate read. Alex lay on his back, keeping to his side of the bed, listening to the sound of a page turning every minute or so. As he began to tire he turned on to his side and rested his hand on her stomach.

'Alex,' she said, a friendly warning.

'Just this,' he said, already sleepy. 'Just so I know you're there.' She didn't say anything and a moment or two later he heard a page turn, and he drifted further, moored all the time to the soft warmth of her stomach through the fabric of the night-shirt.

That was how he fell asleep, quickly and without any uneasiness, comfortable in knowing she was there with him. He woke in the early hours though, and couldn't get back to sleep again. He lay there in the dark and listened to Kate's shallow breathing and let his thoughts stray too far.

He began to worry about Natalie. Maybe he'd been too quick to assume she'd followed his advice and disappeared somewhere. After all, she'd been sceptical the same way Rob had. Possibly she'd talked about lying low just to appease him and had actually continued with her daily routine, opening herself up to danger without realizing it.

He'd come here looking for Matt and for all he knew Matt was already engaged in the next stage of his operation, air-brushing Natalie from the picture: a road accident perhaps, or on the tube. There seemed too many ways of killing someone and making it look like an accident, a random death.

Then he thought of what Natalie had said about Matt, and a

counter-argument started to form in his head, the familiar descent back towards a scathing condemnation of his own paranoia. It almost shamed him that he thought of himself as so loyal and yet was willing to think Matt a murderer.

He eased carefully from the bed without disturbing Kate, standing still at the bedroom door to listen out for the faint seashore breaths of her sleep. She always slept well, something he wouldn't have even noticed ten years ago but that he envied now, more than he envied anything else.

He went into the kitchen and poured himself a glass of water, drinking only a few mouthfuls before leaving it on the counter. He walked through to the living room without turning the light on, making his way tentatively around the furniture and to the window.

The wind had dropped but there was still a cold blast of air as he opened the window and leaned out. He felt more real, more solid now, his body taut against the cold, bracing itself. He put that down to Kate. He'd hardly touched her and yet just being with her was bringing him back to the world.

There were fewer lights in the buildings across the street and no one walking below but the atmosphere and the sound of the city were almost the same as they had been earlier in the evening. Each end of the street still sounded busy with traffic, alive.

He hadn't checked the time and wondered now if it was earlier than he'd thought. His heart sank slightly at the prospect, conscious that he'd be tired all through the following day if he didn't get back to sleep. And he didn't want to be tired when he got to Garrington, whether Matt was there or not.

He closed the window and lay on the sofa for a while, drifted in and out of sleep a couple of times but only in short bursts.

Finally, he put one of the table lamps on and took a book of short stories off the shelf – young American writers – working his way through it until he heard Kate's alarm go off.

There was a view through the window now, a grey dawn breaking. He put the book down on the coffee table and went to the bedroom, almost walking straight in but stopping himself and knocking first, waiting for her bemused invitation to come in.

She was sitting up in bed with the lamp on, smiling as she said, 'You're up early.' She looked concerned then and added, 'You didn't have a bad night?'

'No, no, just the jet lag kicking in. What sleep I had was really good.' He liked the way she looked in the mornings, her hair messy and unkempt, her face always surprisingly fresh. 'Does the no sex rule mean I can't give you a good morning kiss?'

'It isn't a no sex rule. I just think we should be careful about not rushing back into things. We need to take our time. Maybe a good morning kiss might be a nice place to start.'

He sat on the edge of the bed and kissed her briefly, holding her then, burying his head in her hair, the faint scent of oranges on it.

'Your hair smells of oranges,' he said, his voice muffled.

'It's not natural, just the conditioner I use.' He laughed and let go of her and she said, 'Do you really think we could get back together?'

'Honestly?' She nodded. 'I hadn't thought that much about it until I got here. I'm not saying I hadn't thought about you. It just seemed like something that was beyond our control.'

'But?'

'Yeah, but. But a lot of things have changed recently, with these deaths, the attacks getting worse.'

She was sidetracked by that, looking concerned as she said, 'Really?'

He nodded. 'Much worse. So I've kind of been thinking for a while now that I needed to do something, put my life in order. Seeing Matt is a part of that but it didn't occur to me that you might be a part of it too, not until last night.' He looked apologetic, for being honest, for finding it so hard to see what had always been there. 'And yet the thing is, it should have occurred to me. That's why the attacks stopped when I was with you – well, almost stopped – because I was happy.'

She looked troubled, the way she'd looked when she'd first seen him the day before.

'Alex, I don't understand.' She shook her head. 'Your attacks didn't stop when you were with me.'

She was wrong. He remembered them stopping, reminding her now.

'Not completely, but they were few and far between. Insomnia, sure, but the sleep paralysis almost ceased. You must remember that it got better?'

She shook her head again and said, 'I remember being woken two or three times a week because you'd just had an attack and flown out of the bed, turned the light on. It used to really scare me just to see the way you looked, the fear on your face, your eyes glaring at me like I was a stranger. And I remember times when I'd look at you during the day and it was as if you couldn't even see me because you were thinking about . . .' She paused and added simply, 'Whatever it is that you dream of.'

He was confused, thrown by the detail of her memory, a memory that should have been familiar to him and yet wasn't. The attacks had almost stopped when he'd been with her, he'd been certain of that, one of the few certainties he'd had left.

'I don't remember. I mean, I remember it differently.'

She didn't say anything but held him again. He felt like crying but didn't want to upset her. Nothing was clear any more, not even the things he'd held on to. He was trying to find out if Matt was a murderer and yet he was losing sight of who he was himself. At the very least though, meeting Matt would fill in some of the blanks.

It had to help because he was pinning his hopes on it now. Whatever the truth behind these deaths, he had to take the good from it, the chance to face up to his problems and question his own part in them. This conflict of memories with Kate was just more proof that he couldn't go on living life as a stranger, to himself, to the people around him, to the women he encountered.

That was the worst of it, that he'd let Natalie go and then Kate. And he was beginning to understand why now, the things Kate had said, that at some deep level he'd never been with them, always holding a part of himself back, one woman in his life poisoning and stunting his relationships with all the others.

13

He hadn't given much thought to his own death over the past few weeks. He understood that if the same person had been responsible for the deaths of both Will and Rob then his life was also in danger. He'd been fearful a couple of times too, the day on the tube in particular.

Even so, his own death hadn't much concerned him. If anything, he'd thought less about it than he had beforehand, his self-pitying suicide fantasies no longer justifiable or even decent.

Perhaps he hadn't thought about it because he hadn't imagined himself among the living in the first place. He was under threat of death, and somehow that just hadn't felt like much of a threat. He'd become detached from life, from the people who could have meant something to him, like a holy man in old age, severing his connections with the world.

Now though, on this train heading north under a darkly leaden sky, he was thinking about death, not as some intangible world that he entered through his sleep but as something violent and final and alien. He didn't want to die, the most basic desire imaginable and yet it had taken seeing Kate again to restore it.

Possibly it had taken a lot of things: the deaths of friends, the brief echo of what he'd shared with them, the gradual realization of what he'd lost. Seeing Kate though, being with her, that had made him see the possibilities of what still lay ahead. He'd lost sight of it over the years, but there were reasons still to live.

It wasn't burning through him, no blinding reaffirmation. The only indication of a change was the steady caution developing between his layers of thought. He needed to be vigilant, to make sure people knew that he was going up to Matt's house, to cover all the angles where some accident might be engineered.

Part of it was staying awake. He'd only been on the train a few minutes when he began to feel his body sliding towards sleep. He needed to stay awake though, and not because of the embarrassment of having an attack in public this time, but for his own safety.

He chatted to a woman across the aisle from him; she was wary at first but took quickly to his accent and his tourist's enthusiasm, recommending places for him to visit and things to do. She left the train at one of the early stops though, giving him a modest wave from the platform.

There were no other people nearby so he read the paper intently, then studied the view through the window. He could feel the need for sleep sweeping in like tidal waters, engulfing him on all fronts. He persevered, aware that he would pass through it, find a path back to wakefulness.

The sound of the train rose and fell and then something crashed through, thumping against the side of the carriage, so loud that it startled him awake and left him shaken. He looked around at the other passengers but no one else seemed to have noticed. Yet something large had hit the side of the carriage above his window.

Possibly it had been something else, a smaller noise within the carriage that had been amplified and twisted, his senses already dislocated by sleep. He couldn't help but look along the top of the window though, convinced that something had hit it with a forceful muffled thump.

The sound had been familiar somehow, instantly recognizable. He shuffled through his memories, stalling as it fell into place. And he knew now that the object hitting the window had been a product of his own mind, a body, wrapped up against the cold in a winter coat.

He tried hard to focus on the real world of the carriage but it had spooked him. Sleep was gnawing at him and he couldn't help but think of her, as if she really had bounced off the side of the train. It was as if she were growing impatient waiting for him to sleep, mounting an assault now on his waking world.

It was sleep, that was all, the need for sleep. Yet he refused to yield, sensing that if she was in the shallows she'd be in the deeps too, waiting for him. He got to his feet instead, walked to the end of the carriage, looking out of the window on one side and then the other, all the time ignoring the troubled stares of the other passengers.

By the time he got to Garrington he'd passed through it again and was experiencing a sleep deprivation high. The taxi driver wanted to tell him everything the village had to offer and Alex engaged happily with him, asking him why it was a village and not a town, what its history was, tourist stuff.

The hotel was small and traditional, on a main street of restaurants and antique shops. He guessed it was low season but there were plenty of people window-shopping, wrapped and padded against the cold. There were a few people sitting around in front of the fire too, in the hotel's large open lobby.

He checked in, made a quick tour of the room and then went back down to the reception and asked for directions to Matt's house. He wanted to check it out before calling, so that he had some idea where he was going, what kind of place.

The receptionist was young and blank and overly made-up, the look of someone who wanted to work for a chain rather than the independent she was in. She smiled and stared at the address before saying, 'Oh, it's not far at all. If you drive right along Main Street—'

'I don't have a car. I'm walking.'

She looked momentarily flummoxed but smiled again as she found a suitable response. 'I can call you a cab.'

'No, thanks, I want to walk, if it's not too far.'

She studied the address again, as if the directions had changed now that he was walking. Finally she nodded to herself, and said, 'That should be fine.' She smiled and pointed, saying, 'Walk right along Main Street, cross the bridge and take a right. That's Riverside Lane.'

'Oh, so it's not far.' She smiled but didn't respond so he thanked her and left.

He felt a little out of place as he walked along Main Street in his overcoat and scarf, most of the other people dressed like they were hikers or ready for winter sports. The further he walked, the less it bothered him, because he was invisible anyway, his reflection passing unnoticed across the windows that people looked in.

Main Street came to an abrupt end with the bridge across the river. He stopped and looked down at the water quite a way below, fast and loud, breaking white over its rocky floor. He looked back the way he'd come then, Main Street looking pretty much like all there was to Garrington.

Beyond the bridge there were a few houses on either side of the road, woods, not much else. Riverside Lane looked at first like it was cut through a woodland that was devoid of houses, climbing slowly away from the town and from the river itself which grew quieter as he walked.

He'd been making steady and isolated progress for ten minutes before he encountered the first gated entrance and a drive leading off to a house that wasn't visible from out there. It was another twenty minutes and three more houses before he came to Matt's.

He slowed but walked past, checking the gates for cameras, glancing beyond to see if anyone was about. He looked up and down the road then to see if any cars were approaching. He was alone out there, leafless branches clattering lightly, a mournful sound beyond which the river was inaudible now.

He crossed the road and walked back to the gates. There was still plenty of greenery on that side, shrubs and hedges to shield the houses from the road. Even so, with the trees bare he could just make out part of the roof of the house, set well back, the drive clearly sweeping away and then back towards it.

There was no sign of anyone about. He kept checking behind him, nervous that he might look suspicious to people passing, but even though there was nothing to see he couldn't move on. He kept staring at the stray edges of gable he could see, trying to picture the house beneath it, the people inside.

He wondered how Matt would react to him if he was there. That was one of the reasons he'd come, because he was certain he'd know from Matt's face alone when he saw him, whether it was him. And if he thought Matt was innocent he could simply play along with the charade of the surprise visit, the sad news of old friends.

That was something he hadn't thought about though, and it troubled him now. He'd considered the possibility of Matt being innocent in all of this, and had thought too of the things he would say to him about that night ten years ago, but he hadn't yet thought of breaking the news about Will and Rob.

It had never occurred to him that if Matt was innocent he

wouldn't know about the deaths. And as he thought of how he'd tell him he realized that he hadn't even thought about the deaths himself.

He'd thought about them in an abstract way, as part of a potentially lethal puzzle he needed to solve, but he hadn't pictured the deaths, imagined those last moments, and wasn't that what people were meant to do? Normal people showed empathy, part of the grieving process which for him had been swept up in more personal concerns.

For the first time he thought of Will, already drugged perhaps, the reason for the lack of a struggle, his killer carefully injecting the lethal dose of heroin into his arm. He thought of him slipping into coma as he lay there, his body growing cold while the only person who cared about him was away for the weekend.

And he thought of Rob, wondering whether he'd gone out on an adrenaline rush, more thrill than nightmare, or whether they'd been scared in those last few minutes as the explosions had crept closer and the walls had shattered around them. He hoped not, uncomfortable with the thought of Rob being scared at the end.

He wanted both of them to have died good deaths, without pain or fear, because in some way it seemed to justify the fact that he'd felt so little, that he still felt so little. They'd been his friends and they were dead; he registered that truth but he didn't know what he was meant to feel, except perhaps that it shouldn't be nothing.

Suddenly he didn't want Matt to be hidden away in the silence beyond those gates. Alex had gone there to confront him and yet now he was more troubled by the thought of Matt seeing what he'd become, a shadow of the person they'd known back at college. Whatever Matt had become, it was hard to believe it could be a worse transformation than his.

A raindrop hit him on the cheek. It was icily cold. He lifted his hand and wiped it away but the rain started to fall heavily and quickly. He looked up at the sky, cloud on cloud, angry and dark. The walk out there had probably taken about forty minutes and he wasn't sure what to do now.

The trees along the road wouldn't provide much cover, and he didn't like the idea of being seen lurking around in the undergrowth. He turned and looked at the gate, the buzzer and intercom on the brick post. Even the briefest contemplation of pressing that button was enough to make him start walking.

He didn't want to see Matt, not yet. He was no longer convinced that he wanted to see him at all but he was determined that he would. He'd prepare himself and he'd call, because for all that it would expose him, he still saw it as the only way. If he wanted to free himself he'd have to see Matt first, and he would see him – just not yet.

He walked away, a brisk pace back down the lane. The rain was heavy and cold but it was driving into his back so it wasn't too bad except when it found a way above his scarf and on to his neck. He'd be soaked through by the time he got back but for the moment he felt fine.

Within ten minutes he was cold and making slow progress. The lane seemed longer than it had and though the slight gradient was in his favour now it didn't make up for the discomfort of being wet. The water was running down from his hair, finding inroads beneath the scarf, the lower part of his trousers soaked through too and sticking to his legs.

He heard a car approaching behind him, the engine quiet but the tyres hissing through the surface water. Alex turned as it got close, making sure the driver had seen him on the edge of the road. It was a police patrol car, slowing down as it reached him, the officer inside staring quizzically at him.

He brought the car to a stop and lowered the window and said, 'Hi.' He was middle-aged, bulky, and appeared to have been rendered almost speechless, as if he'd encountered an extraterrestrial or some character from an urban legend.

'Hi,' said Alex. 'I was out for a walk, but I'm afraid I should have checked the weather forecast.'

The policeman smiled now as if it all made sense, and said, 'You're a tourist.'

'Yes, that's right. I'm staying at the Furloe on Main Street.'

'Get in. I'll take you back.'

'Thanks.' Alex walked around the car and got in. 'This is very kind. I feel stupid for being out here. I'm Alex Stratton by the way.'

'Jeff Clinton – no relation.' He smiled and drove off. 'You could've been dressed better but you never can tell when the rain's gonna come. What brings you to Garrington?'

Alex wanted to tell him, for the insurance it would provide and for any information Jeff might have about the family. But he couldn't tell him now, guessing Jeff might know the MacAndrews or know of them. Alex had already told him he was just out for a walk so it would seem suspicious.

At the same time he wanted to given an impression of himself as a normal person. Since the day on the tube he'd been conscious of the possibility of a death that looked like suicide, conscious too of the people who'd line up to agree that his behaviour had been odd. He didn't want to add a police-man to the number.

'Antiques,' he said. 'I'm visiting a friend in New York but I've just come up for a couple of days to check out the antique shops.'

Jeff glanced over at him, taking in again the overcoat, the look of him. Alex could see that it all added up in Jeff's mind, that he was curious rather than suspicious.

'That's what brings a lot of people. You seen anything you like?'

'Couple of things. I haven't shown too much interest yet though; it pays to keep them guessing.'

'You got that right.'

They were already approaching the bottom of the lane. Alex felt like the water had worked through his overcoat where his back was pressed against the seat and in the warmth of the car he felt damp and musty. He continued to chat breezily though, as Jeff drove him the final stretch along Main Street which was deserted now.

Alex thanked him when they got to the Furloe and Jeff wished him luck with his antique-shopping. He went in then, the area by the fire quite crowded now and noisy with four or five different conversations going on. The same receptionist gave him a smile, apparently failing to notice that he looked like he'd been swimming in his clothes.

He took a shower and ordered soup and sandwiches from room service, sitting in his robe as he ate them, no light on, the daylight failing to struggle past the window and into the room. It was already growing dark anyway, the gloom merely heightened by the weather that had swept in over the past hour.

He tried to call Kate but she wasn't in yet. He sat with the phone on his lap then, telling himself to dial Matt's number but not doing it. If he didn't make that call there was no reason for him to have come to Garrington but he was nervous about doing it, and not because of some intangible fear for his own safety.

The real apprehension lay elsewhere, in the fear that everything that had happened over the past few weeks had been shaped and fashioned by his diseased imagination. What he feared most from this meeting was a realization of his descent into confusion and paranoia.

Matt would smile and be friendly, but he'd be puzzled that someone he hardly remembered had come all this way just to surprise him. And as Alex stuttered and stumbled through his recollection of their joint past Matt would grow increasingly uncomfortable, sensing that this friend's spirit had crumbled, wondering how they could ever have been friends in the first place.

Part of what had brought Alex here was the need to tell him things about that night, things that he thought it important for Matt to know, but maybe Matt didn't want to know. Like Rob had said, Matt had probably long brushed off any memory of that night. Maybe. Sitting there now he couldn't even remember who Matt was, let alone imagine who he'd become.

He put the phone back, switched on the bedside lamp and walked over to the window. It had stopped raining though the sky still looked threatening. There were people walking along the street again, lights from shops and from passing cars. The thought of the night ahead dragged his mood down into the shadows.

He thought back to hearing that thump against the side of the train and was astonished at the ingenuity of the tricks his own mind played on itself. He let his focus shift then from the street to the faintly lit image of the room behind him and imagined briefly the stirring of air, the reflected face, the movement seen from the corner of his eye.

It was enough to spur him into action. He drew the curtains and got dressed. He sat back down on the edge of the bed then and picked up the phone, dialling the number without giving himself the chance to put it off again. It had hardly rung at the other end when a woman answered.

'Hello?' She sounded puzzled, as if already owed an explanation for the call.

'Hi, is this the MacAndrew house?'

'Yes, who's calling please?' She sounded young, not Matt's mother but his sister perhaps; Alex remembered him having a younger sister.

'My name's Alex Stratton. I was a friend of Matt's at college. It's out of the blue, I know, but I wondered if you had contact details for him, or if he was there now.'

There was a pause, perhaps long enough for a quick silent consultation, and then she said, 'No, he isn't here.' She paused again. 'Look, why don't you come over?'

'Well, I don't want to bother you if . . .' He stumbled to a halt as he realized what she'd just said. She knew he was there, in Garrington. 'How do you know I'm nearby?'

The puzzled tone was there again as she said, 'Caller ID.'

'Oh, I see.' He felt now like he needed to explain why he was there and so he resurrected the story he'd told Jeff Clinton. 'Yeah, I'm visiting a friend in New York – New York City, I mean – and I came up here to look at antiques, so I thought while I was in the neighbourhood . . .'

'I understand. I'll expect you shortly then.' He agreed and said goodbye but something was troubling him about the way she'd sounded, as though she wasn't being straight with him, or as though she'd been expecting his call, something in her tone that he couldn't quite pin down. She talked too as though she were alone in the house but he'd got the feeling she wasn't, those pauses, the feel of someone standing in the background.

He went down to reception and got them to order a cab from there. He was relieved to see a different receptionist, a middle-aged woman who engaged with him and took note of where he said he was going, saying even that she knew where the house was.

He'd do the same in the cab too, ask the driver for a card, tell him to expect a call later in the evening for the return leg. It was unlikely Matt would try to pull anything there on his own doorstep but it did no harm to be cautious. Possibly it did no harm to be paranoid either.

14

It was late afternoon by the time the cab took him back across the bridge and up Riverside Lane. He sat in the back and the driver didn't seem much inclined to talk so Alex just looked out of the window, at the lit shops and houses and then at the velvet darkness of the woods.

When they got to the gate the driver pulled up so that he could lean out of his window to press the buzzer for the intercom. He looked at it expectantly, ready to speak, but the gates started to open without anyone asking who was there. He shrugged to himself and leaned back in.

'Actually,' said Alex, 'I'll get out here and walk up.'

'Okay,' said the driver, implicit in his tone that Alex could suit himself. Alex paid him and asked for a card but the driver said, 'All the cards have gone. We're in the book.'

'Oh. Well, I'll call later then, when I'm ready to come back.'

'You have a nice evening,' said the driver, the sound of his voice suggesting again that he didn't really care what kind of evening Alex had or whether he'd be calling later.

Alex walked up the drive, slowing to adjust to the darkness as he moved away from the lamplight of the gates. The rain had stopped and he could see patches of dark sky between the raggedly broken clouds, a couple of stars. The wind had dropped too, and he could hear the river again and the sound of rainwater still dripping from the leaves and branches of the garden.

As the drive swung back on itself he got his first proper view of the house. It was big, lots of brick and timber beams, a too-perfect interpretation of an English country house. There was a light on in the porch and a couple more lamps but the house itself looked to be in darkness.

Maybe the woman he'd spoken to was alone after all, or there with just one other person, Matt perhaps. He didn't get the feeling somehow that his parents were there. It had the feel of a house that had been left in the charge of a caretaker, a closed-up and lifeless quality.

He was still a distance from the house when the front door opened, a deeper and warmer light spilling through it. A moment later a woman stepped out and looked down the drive towards him. All he could see at first was a tall slim outline, dark hair.

He thought she was wearing a short dress but as he got closer he saw that it was a long sweater over pale fitted trousers. He could see now that she was Matt's sister too, the same startling blue eyes and pale skin, the same thick curls of hair, hers worn long and high-maintenance.

Alex was smiling but she looked slightly confused and spoke first, saying, 'Where's your car?'

He almost stopped and looked behind him, thrown by the question. 'I don't have one. I came in a cab.'

'You should have said. I would have come over for you.' She smiled now, putting out her hand as he got close enough. They shook hands like people being introduced for the first time but then she said, 'I don't suppose you remember but we used to write to each other.'

It was true, he'd forgotten, but it came rushing back out of the past now, Matt's younger sister, who'd started to write messages to Alex at the end of her letters to her brother. And a few times, too, Alex had written to her at the end of Matt's letters. She'd been eleven or twelve, something like that, a little kid far away.

'I do remember. Martha.' She smiled. 'It's a little strange though, someone I remember as a little kid being a good few inches taller than me.'

'I wasn't so little even then.' She noticed the bruise on his temple but looked away as if embarrassed. She glanced around briefly, taking in the weather and the turn of the night, then back at him. 'Come inside. You must be cold.'

He followed her into the house, lit by lamps but a long way from the dark interior he'd imagined. She led him into a large living room where a fire was burning and offered him a seat on one of the sofas.

'Can I get you a drink? A Macallan?' He smiled, trying to read her expression and decipher what she'd said. Did she know about him drinking Macallan, something Matt had told her, or just a coincidence perhaps?

'That'd be great.' She crossed the room and poured one for each of them. 'I take it Matt isn't here at the moment?'

'I'm here on my own.' She came back and gave him his drink, then sat on the edge of the sofa facing him, her long frame hunched over her drink, as if she wanted to make herself small again. She sipped at it and Alex followed suit, savouring the warmth of the whisky in his mouth. She looked pensive.

Alex said, 'Is something wrong?'

'No.' She smiled again but more as reassurance. He could tell something wasn't right but still couldn't put his finger on it. 'I'm sorry if I sounded a little odd when you called earlier.'

'You didn't. And anyway, it was probably an odd call to take.'

She paid no attention to his answer, saying instead, 'My

parents are away on vacation. I just came up for a couple of weeks while they're away. There are people here during the day but they like to know someone's actually staying here.' Alex nodded, not sure where this was going. He looked at the blazing fire and the neat stack of chopped logs, the look of the place in general speaking of those people who were around during the day. 'I've got a place in the city, so, you see, I wouldn't usually have been here to take your call.'

'Oh, right,' said Alex, pretending that he understood now. She frowned a little, perplexed, and he realized she was still struggling towards the point she was trying to make.

'I come home all the time but being here alone makes you take stock of life, your childhood, things like that. And then you called.' She looked at him and he smiled a little, showing now that he didn't quite understand what she was getting at. She nodded as if accepting that she needed to get to the point and said, 'I wish you could have found out another way. Matt's dead. He killed himself.'

Alex could still feel that slight baffled smile stuck to his face, the remnant of the final thought before his brain had frozen. He looked at her; she was waiting for a response. He tried to think but it was as if the words existed in some other reality, as if they'd just been spoken on a daytime soap or in a film.

Then the dam burst and overwhelmed him with stray thoughts, questions, panic, confusion. Matt was dead. He'd killed himself. So maybe he wasn't behind this, but if it wasn't him who else could it be? Should he tell her that Matt might not have killed himself but been murdered? Matt was dead. Dead. She didn't seem too upset, and her parents were on vacation when their son had just killed himself.

'Your parents went on vacation?'

'Yes.' She couldn't see the point of the question but thought

Kevin Wignall

it over for a second or two and said, 'Oh, I'm sorry, I should have said. This wasn't recent. It was seven years ago. He connected a tube to the tailpipe of his car. In the garage. The gardener found him.' Alex thought of him sitting in his car, losing consciousness, the mind-numbing irony of him choosing that way out.

'Seven years ago?'

She nodded.

The barrage of questions was still going on in the back of his head, speculating on what it meant now that Matt was out of the picture. It was overshadowed though, by the realization that someone he'd once thought of as one of his closest friends had sunk into a suicidal despair and killed himself within three years of their last meeting. And the worst of it was that none of them had even known.

'I can't believe it,' he said. 'Not Matt; it wasn't his style.' He couldn't believe either that he wouldn't have the chance now to tell Matt the things he'd wanted to tell him about the night they'd hit Emily Barratt. It was all too late. Everything was always too late. The time he'd needed to speak to Matt was seven years ago, the thought taking shape that they'd let him down. 'We should have been there for him.'

She took a sip of her whisky and produced a heavy sigh. She was irritated perhaps, and had the right to be. Here he was, one of her brother's best friends from college, expressing regret and remorse seven years after the fact. It wouldn't help her either to know that what he really felt was shame for not having been there, and shame too for having even considered Matt a murderer.

She sat back and rested her elbow on the arm of the sofa, playing with her hair as she said, 'I have to be honest, Alex, I was pretty angry for a few years about that, angry with all of you. He was a different person when he came back from England – sad, withdrawn. Mom and Dad tried plenty of times to find out what it was that was bringing him down but he'd just closed himself off. And I often wondered why he never heard from any of you. I even asked him once and he told me you were probably all busy getting established and it was only natural. Of course, I didn't think it was natural at all, to have friends who never wrote or called.'

'You're right, it isn't natural, but if it's any consolation, it wasn't just Matt. None of us spoke to each other, and until recently we still hadn't, not for the best part of ten years.'

She looked at him, clear from her eyes that she found no consolation in that fact, and said, 'Maybe so. But I only saw it from Matt's point of view, the fact that when he needed his friends they weren't there. And maybe the rest of you didn't need that friendship but Matt did.'

Alex thought briefly of Will. They'd all needed real friendship more than they'd known, but Matt had clearly needed it most. Perhaps memory played tricks on them too, because if it had been such a great friendship how could it so easily have withered and died? No accident, however tragic, could have done that on its own.

'He never talked about what it was that had brought him low?'

'No.' She looked at him suspiciously, and Alex realized his question had come close to admitting he might have some idea himself.

Before she could throw it back at him he said, 'Did he leave a note?'

She nodded and said, 'I kept it. I told Mom and Dad I burned it because I didn't want them dwelling on it. I kept it though.'

'You don't have it with you?'

'It's in my apartment, but I can tell you what it says if that's what you want to hear. I know every word of it.'

'No, I'm sorry, I . . .'

He was embarrassed for asking but she was determined he'd hear it.

'Dear Mom, Dad and Martha, I hate myself for putting you through this but there's no other way. I want to sleep, that's all, just sleep and be finished with it. Thanks for everything, and I'm sorry it didn't work out the way it should have done. Please don't feel bad. Matty.' Her face was tight with restraint and when she spoke again she sounded angry. 'Not quite as eloquent as you might have expected from Matt, not offering much in the way of answers either, but then, I don't suppose his mind was exactly at its sharpest.'

Alex looked down into his drink. He felt like he was contaminating this house and her life and her memory of Matt just by being there. When he looked up again she was still staring at him, eyes unflinching, demanding some response, as if she'd waited all this time for an encounter like this and wasn't willing to let it go.

Alex stared back and said, 'I don't know what I can say to you. I should have been here but I wasn't. I should have been a better friend but I wasn't. I've never been in the position you're in now but I can't imagine you want to hear my condolences, not now, and you don't want to hear how much he meant to me.'

She laughed bitterly and said, 'No, you're right, I don't. What I'd like to know is what happened. Why did the Matt I'd known shut down like someone had turned off the lights? Why didn't you keep in touch with him? Something happened. All I want to know is what. I don't think that's too much to ask.'

Alex shook his head, thinking of his own empty thoughts of suicide, and said, 'Nothing bad enough to kill himself.' At least it wouldn't have been if they'd kept in touch, helped each other, stayed strong. Like Rob had said, they'd been shallow, just not shallow enough. And perhaps finally the time had come to reject who they'd been then, and the flawed decisions they'd made. 'The five of us were out one night in a car. Matt was driving. He'd had a few drinks but he was okay. A girl, a student, ran in front of the car. She was killed. Matt had been drinking but it hadn't been our fault, so we decided not to go to the police. We kept it secret, and we shouldn't have done. We agreed never to tell anyone.'

Will had probably told people though, and maybe the others too, certainly if Will and Rob had been murdered; but he couldn't be sure of that any more. For a while, with a transformed Matt playing the bogeyman, absurd thoughts and fears had come to make sense. What was he to believe now? That Natalie was the killer, or that he was behind it all himself?

Martha had looked resolute until now. On the surface at least, she was still composed but she looked as if she'd crumpled up inside from a blow.

'I'm sorry,' he said. 'I shouldn't have come here. If I'd known, I wouldn't have done. I'm sorry.'

She shook her head in response but didn't speak and though she wasn't crying he saw for the first time that she was struggling to keep her emotions in check. Finally, she took a deep breath and said, 'You've no idea how much it means just to be told something, to have some understanding of what must have been going through his mind. It's not knowing that really hurts.'

For the first time in years, Alex thought of Emily Barratt's family. They'd never been told the truth either, and maybe a decade on, the pain of her loss and the added pain of not knowing how it had happened was as fresh and raw as it had ever been. Yet at the time, they'd hardly thought of her as having a family at all.

'It wasn't his fault,' said Alex, thinking aloud. 'I came here to tell him that.' He stopped, conscious again of how far his timing was off.

Martha smiled though, and said, 'If he was so racked with guilt I don't think it would have made much difference what you'd told him.' She paused before adding, 'You see, you were wrong, what you said about him, because I know it would have been enough for Matt to kill himself. He was drink-driving and he killed a girl, and he didn't even own up, take the blame. In a way, that would have been the worst of it for Matt, that he'd never owned up. I'm less amazed now that he killed himself, than that he managed to live with a secret like that for three years.'

Alex was thrown by the starkness of hearing the truth spoken like that. It hadn't been a few drinks, Matt had been drink-driving, and they'd killed somebody and hadn't admitted responsibility, not even to themselves. He thought back to his own part in persuading Matt not to go to the police, the memory too painful though.

'We should have gone to the police,' he said. 'Matt wanted to, but we talked him out of it. We thought it was all about friendship, and yet, of course, that was the first thing to go.'

She looked at him with a sudden realization and said, 'Is this why you all lost contact with each other?'

He nodded. 'Partly. I'm sure people lose touch after college anyway but . . .'

'But you were such close friends.' He nodded again and she

smiled and said, 'Come with me. There's something I want to show you.' She got up, putting her drink down on the table. He did the same and followed her out of the room and up the stairs. 'Mom and Dad kept his room the way it was. We gave his clothes to the Good Will but they couldn't bear to change his room.'

'It's understandable I suppose.' She turned briefly and looked at him, as if reading his expression or maybe just to let him know that there was no need for platitudes.

'Of course it's understandable.'

She led him along the landing and opened the door to the bedroom, turning on the light as they walked in. At first glance it was hard to see it as the shrine he'd imagined. It was just a large room with a double bed, a large desk over by the window, a small sofa. It didn't look like a particularly personal space.

He began to notice the details then. There were bookshelves on the wall behind the door, the books thumbed and used, loved. On the desk too there were personal items. It was from the desk that Martha picked up a small picture in a pale wooden frame. She held it out to Alex and said, 'This is what I wanted to show you.'

He stared down at it and smiled, an instant responsive happiness, quickly overwhelmed. It was the five of them, Natalie in the middle between Alex and Will, Rob and Matt on either flank. They were all smiling at the camera, wearing summer clothes, their arms linked over each other's shoulders. He couldn't remember who'd taken the picture for them but he remembered it being taken.

'This was the summer of our first year. We'd just finished our exams. I can't believe how young we look.' He couldn't believe how close they looked either, how happy. He looked at Matt, slouching down slightly to be more on a level with the rest of them, the smile of someone who was completely content.

He'd never thought before, how brave it had been for Matt to go to another country to study, and what a relief it must have been to have made friends like that, to have found a place where he'd felt at home. And it tore at his heart now to think that Matt had kept this picture framed on his desk for three years, the final three years, a reminder of the past that could only have added to his sickness.

He couldn't help but think of him, sitting there suffering the kind of decline that would eventually make suicide an attractive option, the photograph reminding him of happier times. Perhaps he'd looked at that picture and waited, for the phone to ring, for a letter to arrive. Even the thought of Matt being alone was too much.

Martha held out a tissue, the sight of it distracting him, drawing his gaze from the photograph and back to her, his expression puzzled.

'You're crying.'

He shook his head, still confused and lifted his hand to his cheek, becoming conscious of the tears only as he touched them. He was surprised then, that it had moved him so much. He was upset and he couldn't even reduce it to a specific, to sorrow for Matt or the others or himself.

All he knew was that it was difficult to look at that picture: five happy kids captured in their first summer as friends. That's all they had been, kids, beneath all their youthful arrogance, innocents with no idea what lay ahead of them or how ill-equipped they were to deal with it.

'It's amazing to think that three of these people are already dead.' He kept looking at it, taking in his own words and the fact of it, that he and Natalie were standing there with people who, unknown to them, beyond their summer smiles, were already dead. He looked up and took a second to register the look of shock on Martha's face. 'I'm sorry, I should have said. That was kind of the other reason I came here, to tell Matt.'

He could feel the lie in his own face but Martha was too stunned to notice.

'What do you mean? Who? Who else died?'

He pointed at Will first, staring into his eyes to see if there was any sign of it, the weakness that was set to bring him down. 'Will died of a drug overdose a few weeks back. And Rob.' He moved his finger along the glass. 'He was a journalist, in Africa mainly but in the Balkans too. He was killed in Kosovo.'

'When?' She was taking it badly, even though these were people she didn't know, people with whom she was still angry.

'Also a couple of weeks ago.'

For a moment it looked like she would make some comment about these two deaths coming so closely together, or about the bad luck that had befallen their whole group, but she steered away again and said, 'I knew Robert Gibson was a journalist. I did a search a year or so ago and came up with a lot of stuff on him and you.' She laughed a little, distancing herself from her own past anger. 'You can imagine how much more bitter I felt when I saw him being all compassionate about the suffering in Africa, and then you, the eminent sleep researcher, helping people with their disorders.'

'I can understand that, but Rob was a complicated person, and if he'd ever dreamed that Matt was in trouble he would have been here. And as for me, I'm not really in the business of making people better. I don't run that type of sleep lab.' He thought about what he'd just said and added, 'Who can say though? I have helped people in the past. Maybe I could have helped Matt.'

She shook her head in sad dissent and took the picture from him, placing it back on the desk, positioned still so that Matt could see it if he was sitting there. Alex looked around the room, a room that there'd been no life in for seven years. How could he have been dead for that long? Matt had been too vital, too full of promise and potential.

'Did you give away all of his clothes? Even that big old black overcoat he wore?'

She smiled and said, 'Isn't it funny? I'd forgotten that coat. He lived in it.' The smile faded with the turn of her words. 'Who knows, maybe some college kid somewhere is wearing it right now.'

'I hope so.'

'Shall we go back down?' He nodded and walked out first, waiting for her as she turned off the light and closed the door.

As they walked the landing back to the stairs Alex said, 'You said you did a search on us. What did you mean?'

She looked embarrassed, some colour rising on her pale cheeks. 'Oh, it's silly, I know. It's just that it's really played on my mind over the years, that none of you had ever tried to get in touch with him, never even been curious, never sent a birthday or Christmas card. So one day curiosity got the better of me and I did a search.'

'How?'

'On the web,' said Martha, sounding surprised that she had to spell it out.

'I see. You can search for people on the web?'

She frowned, bemused, and said, 'Of course. You go to any search engine and type in the name of the person you're looking for, then sift through the responses to figure out which one's yours. How can you not know this?'

He laughed and said, 'I use the web for work. I knew you

could do searches, but I have to be honest, it's never occurred to me to search for information about people I know. You can even get information about regular people?'

'It helps if they have a reason to be mentioned somewhere or other but you'd be surprised how many people are mentioned. Come to the study and I'll show you.' He followed her, wondering what he could have found out about the others, perhaps even about Emily Barratt, simply by tapping their names into a search engine.

The first name she brought up was his own and suddenly the screen was full of links to pages, most of them related to sleep research institutes and publications. There was no surprise there, nor when she put Rob's name in, plenty of links to Rob's work in amongst the links to the lives of all the other Robert Gibsons.

She typed Will's name in and sighed a little.

'I didn't get anywhere with this one. There are too many William Shaws, too many different things. I thought one of them could easily be him but I had no way of knowing which one.'

Alex looked at them, baseball players, financial analysts, a Shaw family homepage. It saddened him as he said, 'Probably none of them was Will.'

She turned and glanced at him briefly and said, 'Matt didn't feature either, and neither did Natalie. At least, she might have done but Natalie Harrison brings up lots of references to genealogical sites.' She was typing as she spoke and the links in question appeared on the screen now, references to a Natalie Harrison who'd married a Francis Jeffers in 1758, another who'd been born in 1801, another who'd died two years earlier, the trails of people searching out their ancestors. Martha leaned towards the screen then and said, 'Oh, wait there, that wasn't there when I searched before. Nor that.' She clicked on a link before Alex had time to read it and a new page appeared on the screen.

It was a page from some kind of society webzine. Martha scanned through the text and Alex said, 'What is it?'

'Nothing,' said Martha, still reading. 'Jerry Brook has announced he's to marry long-time girlfriend Natalie Harrison next summer. He's the next likely governor of Kentucky, tipped as a future President – lowlife. It's hardly likely to be the same Natalie Harrison. Oh, she is English though, a futures analyst.'

She pointed at the screen and Alex said, 'Can you get a picture of her?'

She looked up at him, doubtful at first but saying, 'I'll look for photographs of Brook and see what we come up with.'

Alex stood looking down at the screen as Martha sat and trawled for pictures of Jerry Brook. He was certain too, that it wouldn't be the same Natalie Harrison but he was edgy as the first picture downloaded on to the screen.

Natalie had teased him about Matt making a run for the Presidency, and she'd told him she was single. They were innocuous comments on their own but they'd develop a sinister edge if she turned out to be the same person they were looking at now.

The first picture showed a guy in his early forties who looked sleek like a salesman. There was a blonde woman with him and they were both dressed for dinner, the picture taken at some fundraiser or charity ball. The woman wasn't Natalie.

'That could be the Natalie Harrison in question,' said Martha, 'but it doesn't say anything in the caption.'

She kept trying, producing a handful of pictures of Brook alone, on a farm, touring a school, a factory, more society pictures, at the opening of some kind of medical facility. Alex took in each of the pictures, conscious of how strange it was that the two of them were doing this together.

They didn't know each other at all and yet they seemed driven in trying to find out if the Natalie Harrison in that photograph upstairs was the same one who was engaged to a politician called Jerry Brook. Alex could understand why he wanted to know, why he needed to know, but not why Martha was so curious.

Another picture started to creep on to the screen and Martha sat back, taking her hands off the keyboard. It was taken at a formal party, Brook on the left talking to an elderly couple on the right, and between them looking on, almost in the shadows, a younger woman. Alex had to look closer this time, studying the face, the hair.

He stood back again and Martha said, 'Is that her?'

'No.' He didn't sound certain and she looked up at him. 'No, it's not a clear picture but I'm positive it isn't her.'

Martha nodded but still didn't look convinced. She turned back to the screen then and said, 'Of course, we don't know that this is the woman he's engaged to anyway. Let's try some more.' She brought up a couple more pictures, none of them offering anything or anyone else, and as she continued searching she said, 'What does your Natalie do?'

'I'm not sure,' said Alex. 'I know she works in the City. She could be a futures analyst I suppose. I just don't know.'

'What company does she work for?'

'I don't know that either. Sorry.'

She gave up on the search, turning to him as she said, 'I don't want you to worry or anything, but you really need to find out if this is the same Natalie Harrison.'

Alex didn't like the sound of this, the way Martha was

homing in on his own fears, even without the benefit of the information he had, the doubts about how Will and Rob had died.

'Why would it matter? Look, I met her at Rob's funeral and she said she wasn't even seeing anyone.'

'All the more reason to check. Two of your friends have died in the last two weeks. If that coincides with a third friend getting engaged to Jerry Brook then I think you have good cause to be uneasy.'

'No,' said Alex, refusing to contemplate it himself, not wanting to hear Martha grasping after the truth either.

She was too quick though, her voice flat but insistent as she said, 'But you were all involved in a hit and run. You killed a girl and left the scene. If that got out it could really damage someone like Jerry Brook, even if it was his wife and not him who'd been involved.'

Alex laughed, the way Rob and Natalie had laughed at him.

'Natalie isn't that kind of person. She wouldn't have someone killed. It's ridiculous.' It did sound ridiculous and yet he thought back to meeting her at Rob's funeral and wondered how well qualified he was to say what she was or wasn't capable of.

'Maybe it isn't her. Maybe all she did was tell the man she loves. Jerry Brook is a real family-values Republican with a fortune and big business links and an uncle who was deputy director of the CIA or NSC or something like that.'

Alex laughed again, more convincing this time as he said, 'I take it you're not a Republican.'

She smiled too and said, 'Granted, we're Democrats but Jerry Brook is still lowlife, and I can assure you that if he knows about the accident you were involved in he'd think nothing of eliminating the people who could point to his future wife being involved. This is politics we're talking about, and, trust me, in this country when it comes to politics no measure is too extreme.'

'This is, of course, if it's the same Natalie Harrison.'

Martha nodded, an edge of sarcasm as she said, 'You're right, I'm sure there are plenty of British futures analysts called Natalie Harrison.'

Alex shrugged, not responding, saying finally, 'Shall we go and finish our drinks?'

'Sure.'

They went back through to the lounge but as soon as they sat down again Martha said, 'I hope you don't think I'm being paranoid about this, Alex, but just as a precaution, I'd recommend you go public in some way. Or leave a deposition with your attorney and let Natalie Harrison know about it. Let Jerry Brook know about it.'

He sighed deeply, just to let her know that he was thinking about it, struggling to get some respite from her needling towards the truth. He took a sip of his whisky then and she did likewise and they sat in silence.

It was the first time he'd encountered someone as paranoid as him and it was throwing his thoughts into confusion. He'd come here thinking Matt had been behind something exactly the same as she was describing. And yet it felt now like the evidence was too circumstantial, and even if it was the same Natalie Harrison he didn't want to believe that she could have come to this.

He thought of Matt's note again and understood it because he just wanted to be able to sleep and forget about it, about everything. He didn't want to consider the possibility that Natalie, or Jerry Brook if he was in fact her boyfriend, might want to have him killed. He wanted to go back to a time before any of this had happened.

The thought made him look up again and at her. He remembered now, the letters, the way she'd talk about what she was doing at school and ask what subjects he was studying. He'd asked her once if she had a boyfriend and received a mortified response that she was too young. A whole correspondence carried out as a footnote to Matt's letters.

'I've become so unbelievably insensitive,' he said, the words coming out as he thought them. She frowned a little, a slight knitting of the eyebrows that he'd noticed a couple of times and found endearing. 'Seriously, this is who I've become. You tell me your brother is dead and I haven't even thought to ask how it's been for you.'

She shook her head dismissively and said, 'He did die seven years ago, and this must have been a shock for you.'

'That's no excuse, because you even told me in so many words that it's been playing on your mind while you've been here alone. And I knew how close you and Matt were. It must have been devastating.'

She didn't answer for a moment, an amazing stillness about her, like a snag in time, and when she spoke again her voice was soft and composed.

'The strange thing was, at the time it didn't seem like such a shock, not to any of us. And he'd been so low, I think we were almost relieved for him. But then the funeral came – that's a long week, waiting for the funeral – and suddenly I couldn't understand why we were burying him. It was like we'd given up on him. I'd forgotten who he was but I saw that casket, that big, big casket, and it made me remember how great he'd been, how I'd idolized him, the way I'd cried when he flew to England for the first time, inconsolable.' She took a sip of her drink but Alex remained silent, feeling like she was only pausing, gathering her thoughts. And it was painful to hear but he owed her this and wanted to hear it too, to be reminded once more who Matt had been. She held the whisky in her mouth for a while before swallowing it and then said, 'I wanted to fix him in my mind but it was too late, he was already dead. It was like I'd dreamt him. Still now, it's like I dreamt him. No one was ever that good, or that great a brother, or that great a person.' Had he been great? Alex couldn't remember well enough, but he was touched that she thought so and couldn't help but question his own chances of receiving a eulogy like that.

'The wrong people die,' he said, aware that it sounded trite but feeling it true all the same. She produced a politely grateful smile and he added, 'And you didn't dream him. He was a better person than I ever was, and I've fallen a long way from my best.'

She looked a little bemused and said, 'You're not a bad person. I don't believe that for a minute.'

'Not bad.' He thought about it for a second. 'I forgot how to live. That's what happened to me, I forgot how to live, how to think about other people and enjoy them.' Simply seeing Kate again had taught him that much, realizing how close he'd come to losing her, the same way he'd lost Natalie years before.

'Well, lucky for you; you're still alive and you've realized that. You have time to make changes.' She paused, as if conscious that she was about to move back into territory where Alex felt uncomfortable. 'Which is why you need to remove this threat, or potential threat.'

He didn't want to talk about it but she was probably right that he needed to be cautious so he said, 'Okay, if it makes you feel better, I'll place something with a lawyer and I'll tell Natalie. Trust me though, Natalie is not the reason Will and Rob died. I have absolute faith in that.' For a moment, too, as he said it he believed it, but he knew that given time he'd begin to doubt her and want to know for sure, the same way he'd come so easily to doubt Matt. Martha smiled, reassured, and he added, 'So let's talk about something else. Tell me about you, Martha. What do you do? What have you been doing since you were that little girl who wrote to me?'

'Oh my.' She finished her drink and got up, holding out her hand for his glass. 'I think we'll need more drinks.'

She told him about Sarah Lawrence, taking a Master's. She was working for a literary agency now but he got the impression it was a recreational job. She was smart and funny once she got into her stride, her sense of humour reminding him of Matt.

And Martha wanted to know about Alex, the usual things people asked him, about sleep research, dreams. She wanted to know what had happened in the years after college too, how and when he'd broken up with Natalie, if he'd spoken to the others at all in the years since.

Alex told her about Rob's funeral, about meeting Rebecca afterwards, and he noticed her eyes moistening as he told the story. It reminded him again of what she'd said earlier, about being back here on her own, thinking of the past.

'I'm sorry,' he said. 'Is this upsetting you?'

'No, not at all. I just think it's really sad, that she felt as if she'd found someone and then he was killed.'

'Oh.' He nodded and thought of another question, leaving a suitable pause before he said, 'Are you seeing anyone?'

'Not at the moment. And you?'

'No. Well, maybe.' He laughed a little, happy just to have thought of Kate again. 'My ex-girlfriend lives in New York. I think we might be getting back together. I don't know. It's too soon to tell.' Two days ago he'd have put money on it never happening and he was filled with optimism that things had fallen into place so quickly, a sign that perhaps he could transform himself if he was determined enough to see it through.

'Will you move to New York?'

'I think we'd prefer somewhere quieter but it's really too soon to tell.'

She smiled and said, 'Who knows, maybe we'll get to know each other properly.'

'I'd like that.'

He yawned, not even aware of it until Martha said, 'Are you tired?'

'God, sorry. I am tired though. I should probably go.'

'Stay here,' she said, more like a plea than an offer. He looked at her and she added, 'There are plenty of rooms, and I can drive you back into Garrington in the morning. I'd like it if you stayed.'

It felt easier to stay than go back to the hotel anyway, but he could see too that she really wanted him there, to have another person sleeping in the house.

'Okay, thanks.'

She smiled and said, 'You can sleep in Matt's room if you like.' Alex looked puzzled at the offer and her smile slipped. 'Of course, not a good idea. I didn't think. We do have guests stay in there sometimes but obviously you don't want to. Honestly, I don't know what I was thinking.'

'No, you're wrong, I'd be happy to stay in Matt's room.'

They went back upstairs and Martha found him a new toothbrush, pointed out where the bathroom was and left him. When he was alone in Matt's room he walked around it slowly, taking in again the faint traces of the person who'd lived there.

Finally he sat at the desk and stared at his own reflection in the window and then at the photograph in the frame. He wanted to be moved again but it was less charged this time. He sat there for a few minutes, waiting for any thoughts to come to him but he was too tired for thinking. He needed to sleep, and everything else was slipping away against that need.

He got undressed and into bed, turning the light out. He thought he could hear the river in the distance but there was no other sound. His mind strayed and he thought back to his nervousness earlier in the day, his fear of sleeping, the sense of Emily Barratt waiting for him to lose his concentration.

She wouldn't come tonight though, he was certain of that. He wasn't sure why but he was convinced she wouldn't come, and as his thoughts slipped away from the logical he began to get a sense of Matt there in the room with him, a benign presence, forgiving, good. Alex was sleeping in the room of someone he'd wronged and neglected, and yet for the first time in years he had no fear at all of the night ahead.

15

The next morning was bright, cloudless. Alex felt refreshed, something he couldn't help dwelling upon as Martha drove him back to the hotel. He'd slept in Matt's old bedroom and had the most restful sleep he could remember in a long time.

A less rational mind might have concluded that Matt had watched over him and kept Emily Barratt at bay. Maybe he'd even thought like that himself the night before; he couldn't really remember, but he entertained the idea now, not because he subscribed to it but because it was a nice thought, comforting.

There were plenty of reasons why he might have slept better but most likely it had just been a coincidence, a good day in the cycle. He didn't even want to invest any hope in one of the other possibilities, that by coming here he'd broken the cycle completely. He'd hoped for that after nearly every good night's sleep in the past ten years, and he'd always been disappointed.

When they got to the hotel Martha said, 'Do you have to go today?'

He nodded regretfully. It wasn't true and in a way he wanted to stay, to get to know her more, to keep her company, to be there the way he hadn't been for her brother. But he felt a more urgent need to get back and be with Kate, to show her that he'd been serious the other night about making a go of it, to keep up the momentum.

'I wish you'd call someone before you leave. If they know you've been here . . .'

Alex put his hand up to stop her and said, 'Martha, I'm quite safe for the moment, believe me. And as soon as I get back to New York I'll post a statement to my solicitor and tell Natalie that I've done it.'

'And Jerry Brook.'

'And Jerry Brook,' he said, though he could see what a crank that would make him look, phoning up someone he didn't know with a message like that. She seemed relieved and they were more relaxed as they said their goodbyes and vague promises of keeping in touch.

Alex was about to walk away into the hotel though when he turned again. She lowered her window and he said, 'Promise me something.'

'What?'

'In the unlikely event that something does happen to me, don't say anything to anybody, don't try to find out. Just leave it. Promise me.'

He regretted saying it almost immediately. Her face fell and she got out of the car, holding on to him, saying, 'Call somebody now. Alex, I can get our attorney to come up to the house. We can make the calls from there.'

He eased her free and tried to offer reassurance.

'I said in the unlikely event, didn't I? Even if someone is trying to kill me, which I seriously doubt, they won't make a move this quickly. But look, I'm serious, I want you to make that promise. Never say anything, for your own safety, if nothing else.'

Her eyes sharpened, the blue turning fierce. She smiled then, as if he were the one who didn't understand what was going on here.

'You said yourself, what you all did wrong back at college wasn't killing that girl – it was keeping it secret. If something happens to you, I'll write an exposé in the *Times*. I have the contacts and I'll do it. That's a promise.'

He smiled, realizing he wouldn't get her to back down and said, 'It won't come to that. And that's a promise too.' He stood up on his toes to kiss her on the cheek and then walked into the hotel without looking back.

On the train home he thought over what he should do next. He'd dismissed it with Martha, not wanting her to worry, but the truth was he had no idea whether Natalie was behind this or not. He wanted to remain sceptical but Martha had been right about one thing: it was a pretty big coincidence if it wasn't the same Natalie Harrison.

But if Natalie was engaged to Jerry Brook, what did that prove anyway, other than that she'd chosen to lie to her ex-boyfriend about it? The whole business with Matt should have driven home to him what both Rob and Natalie had already told him, that he was paranoid, seeing danger where there was none, imagining demons.

Martha had been upset, given a week on her own to dwell on the loss of her brother, that past brought into her home then, talk of more deaths. It was hardly surprising that she'd become fearful for Alex's safety but that was hardly a good measure of whether he was really in danger or not.

And despite that, as the journey went on, he decided at least to treat it as a theoretical risk, determined not to make the same mistake Rob had possibly made. He'd find out if Natalie was engaged and then he'd confront her, ask her why she'd lied.

He wouldn't necessarily get the truth of course. He didn't remember Natalie being a good liar, a woman he still thought of as emotionally transparent. Yet if she'd known about Will's death and Matt's she'd done an impressive job of concealing it at Rob's funeral. He'd have to be prepared for more of the same.

Above all, he had to remain open to the possibility of Martha being right. If they were both simply being paranoid then maybe he'd lose a friend he'd only just found again. But if they were right – if they were right she'd never been a friend in the first place and the picture on Matt's desk contained a lie.

He got a taxi from Grand Central to Kate's building. There were plenty of people out on her street. It was too cold to be sitting around but the sun was shining and people were making something of it, walking idly, a couple of people talking like they hadn't seen each other in a while.

He pressed the buzzer and after waiting a few seconds checked his watch, realizing he should have taken the cab to Columbia instead. He looked around and up at the blue sky and decided to walk. If he walked to the corner and imagined himself coming from her old apartment he'd probably get his bearings and find his way.

He headed towards the traffic noise, though it didn't seem so bad once he got there, and now that he was on the corner he felt like he knew where he was. He set off, tightening his grip on his overnight bag as he walked the busier street, meeting the faces as they passed.

A little way on he turned again on to a slightly quieter street and was more relaxed as he walked, taking in the coffee shops, book and record stores. There was jazz playing in a second-hand record store that he thought he remembered going into with Kate the last time he was there.

The people here looked more like students, a good atmosphere. Near the end of the street he came to a second-hand bookstore and stopped to look in the window. There were some bookshelves outside but the prize finds were stocked in the window and he studied them for a few minutes.

Tattered copies of Edgar Allan Poe, Walt Whitman, Stephen Crane, sixties paperbacks of Truman Capote and Norman Mailer, magic books with a promising look of the arcane about them, none of them priced. He considered going in to buy something for Kate but thought better of it. Perhaps it would be nicer to go back together, encourage her to choose something herself.

He could imagine them browsing in there for an hour or more. She'd see something she liked and he'd buy it for her and they'd stroll along the street to one of the coffee shops, letting the afternoon drift by, deciding with no hurry what they'd do that evening.

He looked back up the street, taking in its laid-back atmosphere. Maybe Kate just found it hard being there alone. If they were together he could imagine them taking to the lifestyle, becoming part of the city. He'd go wherever she wanted though, because for him anything was better than where and who he was now.

He turned to carry on his way and saw a young guy walking towards him. For a moment Alex wasn't sure which way he was heading, into the shop or past Alex and along the street. They both seemed to second-guess each other in the wrong direction and Alex smiled and said sorry.

The guy didn't smile back. He came close to bumping into Alex but sidestepped him at the last second, and then Alex felt a twinge on the side of his neck, like he'd been stung or hit by a pellet. It wasn't painful but made him shudder and he looked around, trying to establish what had happened. It had been so quick, too quick even for him to remember what he'd looked like, just someone young, scruffy denims, messy hair.

He could feel something wet now around his collar and lifted his hand to it, a weakening shock surging through him as he felt the warm liquid pumping from the wound in his neck. He could feel himself falling, heard a woman scream, a hammer blow as his head landed on the paving stone.

The guy had sliced his neck with a blade. Alex lifted his hand above his face and looked at the blood that coated it. It had happened too quickly, no time to reflect. He could feel the blood sliding out of him into a pool on the sidewalk, imagined it encircling him, deep crimson, shining like plastic.

A woman's face appeared above him, desperate, frantic. He didn't know whether he was smiling but he felt like he smiled, because she had brown curls of hair, a face like one of da Vinci's angels. He felt her press something hard against the side of his neck, the sensation unpleasant, smothering.

People had come out of the bookshop perhaps because she turned her head and shouted, 'Call 911! And get me some ice! From the coffee shop. Get me ice!' She looked back at him now, into his eyes as she said, 'Stay with me. What's your name?'

'Alex,' he said, but she didn't seem to hear him.

'What's your name?'

'Alex.'

This time she heard him and said, 'Okay, Alex, stay with me.' She was beautiful, and she wanted him to live, like she knew him and he meant something to her, a stranger. 'Stay with me, Alex. I'm gonna get some ice and put it on your neck.' She looked away and screamed, 'Where's that fucking ice?' He thought he heard someone call back.

He tried to think. This was it. He was about to die and he wanted to think but he couldn't; the thoughts wouldn't come. He'd thought for too long anyway, and now that it was happening he felt calm. Maybe that was the way Matt had felt, and the others, maybe Emily Barratt.

He felt a jolt go through him and gasped. His eyes had been open but he hadn't been able to see anything. Now though, he was looking at the young woman again and she was saying, 'It's okay, Alex, that's the ice. I've put ice on your neck to try and slow the bleeding. Now you have to stay with me. Stay with me. The ambulance is on its way.'

'What's your name?' He couldn't hear his own words clearly and neither could she but she knew he'd spoken. She leaned in closer and he said it again.

She leaned away again and said, 'My name's Jennifer.' She was crying now and it upset him.

He wanted to tell her to stop, that he wasn't worth crying over, but he couldn't, too many words.

'It's okay,' he said, but even that didn't seem to reach her. It was as if he were lost somewhere deep inside his own body.

'Stay with me, Alex. The ambulance is coming.' The pitch of her words was escalating each time she used them. He wasn't staying with her, he was slipping away. He was dying and the only things she had to save him were those words and the ice pressed against his neck, neither of them enough.

He had the sense there was a small crowd around him now but he couldn't see any of them. All he could see was Jennifer, crying and helplessly determined. And beyond her he could see the wiry branches of a tree, like the blue sky had cracked, shattering, needing only one more blow to bring it crashing in. He wanted to tell her, look, Jennifer, look up at how amazing this sky is with the tree against it.

'The ambulance is coming. Hear it, Alex? The ambulance is coming. You're gonna be okay.'

He felt like he smiled again. He could hear a siren, the first siren he'd heard on this visit and it was calling for him. Natalie had killed him; that thought came at him suddenly, a moment of lucidity. Natalie had killed him, and now she was alone in the photograph, and he hoped Martha wouldn't say anything, because Natalie was alone and that was enough. If she'd killed him, that was enough.

He heard Jennifer's voice and the siren growing louder, but it was too late. He'd known it was too late as soon as it had happened. There was not time left to make things right with Kate or tell his family how much he loved them, or to tell Matt that it hadn't been his fault.

Another burst of lucidity hit him. Matt was dead. They were all dead. His body was being moved, clattering noise, male voices and a young woman crying, wailing. It was Jennifer and this would be her day, that she had tried to save someone and failed. Perhaps it would become part of the rest of her life.

He wanted to tell her to stop crying, and to forget. He wanted to tell her that it was okay for him to die, that he was where he belonged, where he'd belonged for the last ten years, the mistakes of the past erased. And above all, he wanted to tell her what mattered most, that there would be no more dreams, that his sleep would be untroubled.

PART THREE

They were laughing in the back and Alex started to laugh too. He wasn't even sure what they were laughing about, something at the party he supposed, but it was infectious. He laughed and then he looked ahead at the road and said, 'Where are we going?'

'I'm not sure,' said Matt. Natalie and Will laughed harder, amused by the possibility of them being lost. 'Won't this road take us back to campus?'

'No, I don't think so.'

Rob leaned forward, and said, 'Take the next right. That'll take you on to that long road with all the trees on it, you know where Sam Collins lives?'

'I thought he lived in Union Street?'

'No, he did, but he moved up here during the summer. Anyway, that'll take us back into the town centre and then we can go back out to campus.'

Rob sat back and Matt and Alex exchanged a bemused look, both pretty certain there was probably an easier way home than going into town first and coming back out. Matt looked happy enough though, and turned up ahead into the long tree-lined street Rob had mentioned.

It was wide and empty, a long gentle curve sweeping in towards the town.

'Go faster,' Natalie said. 'Faster, faster.' Matt put his foot down and got a jubilant response from her. He smiled and Alex noticed they were still only doing forty. It felt faster and Natalie was happy.

He liked the way she got drunk. She was never completely out of her head. She seemed to hit merry halfway through the evening and then stay there. The first few times he'd seen her like that he'd wondered if she was putting it on but it was genuine, he knew that now.

'I've never been here,' said Alex, just for something to say.

Matt kept his eyes on the road but said, 'No, nor me.' Alex waited for some comment from the back but there was silence. Maybe they were getting tired.

Something moved near the edge of the road. Alex tried to see what it was but before he could even process the initial movement it had catapulted out into their path. He shouted something but wasn't certain what and then the figure was in front of the car, a person running.

Matt shouted too. It looked for a second like she'd made it past the front of the car but then she flew upwards, like a gymnast leaping through a floor exercise. She hit Matt's side of the car with a sickening thump, muffled, hard, and for a second Alex saw her face tear past, chalk pale. And then she was gone.

Matt hit the brakes, too late. A brief burst of shocked expletives gave way to silence as the car came to a stop, and then Will said, 'What the fuck was that?' He already sounded panicked, like he knew exactly what it had been and what it meant.

Matt turned to Alex and said, 'There was no way I could have stopped.'

'I know,' said Alex. 'She came out of nowhere.' The three in the back all started talking at once and Alex turned in his seat and said, 'Okay, stay calm. I'll go back there and see if she's hurt.'

'Of course she's fucking hurt,' said Rob, laughing slightly but in shock now.

'Oh, Jesus!'

'Stay calm,' said Alex, aiming it at the three of them in the back, conscious that Matt seemed to be holding it together. 'I'll be back in a minute.'

Alex got out of the car, looked up the street behind them and started walking, taking deep breaths of the cold air like it was pure oxygen, listening to his own steps on the road surface and the faint sound of the engine turning over behind him. He was looking hard into the darkness, at the road ahead and along its shadowy edges.

He couldn't see anything. He looked back and tried to calculate how far they'd travelled after hitting her. The impact had been too hard for her not to be here. He couldn't believe she'd walked away from it but he was still walking and he couldn't see anything on the road.

He heard the noise of a car door opening behind him and turned. It was Matt. Alex watched as he got out of the car and inspected it. After a quick check Matt looked up the road and saw Alex and shrugged theatrically before making a more detailed inspection.

It was like they hadn't really hit someone at all. That was what Matt had to be thinking and from where Alex stood it was looking that way too. He tried to think whether it was possible that they'd seen it wrong, that perhaps she had made it past but had thumped the car in anger.

It was impossible though. He'd seen her hit the car twice, fly into the air like she'd been yanked up by wires, like a stage trick. Alex turned and kept walking and almost immediately felt sickened. There was a body lying in the middle of the road up ahead.

He picked up his pace and within a few seconds he was standing over her. He couldn't believe she'd been thrown so far. She was lying on her back, and he guessed the back of her head was smashed in because there was a pool of blood forming around it.

She was dead, he knew it. Her eyes were closed, her face perfect and reposed, as if she'd fallen asleep there, nothing more. He knelt down and tentatively put his hand on her neck. He couldn't find a pulse but kept his hand there for a second or two anyway, hoping.

He tried to look at the underside of her head, grimacing at the sight of it. It looked really bad, her hair swimming in blood. He wondered if that had killed her or the impact of the car – not that it mattered. He sat back on his heels and looked at her, trying to think what to do, distracted then by a smell that was coming off her.

What was it? Something sweet, peaches perhaps. Peach schnapps. He looked at her body and noticed the liquid-dark patch around the pocket of her winter coat. He carefully pulled the edge of the pocket, the smell growing stronger, the broken glass grating in the confines of the pocket.

She'd been carrying a bottle of schnapps in her pocket, a half bottle by the look of it. He wondered if she'd been at the same party as them. He looked around too at the half-hidden houses, wondering if she'd come from one of them, why she'd been running, if something had panicked her.

She looked like a student but he didn't recognize her. He looked at her face again and was mesmerized by how beautiful she was, so beautiful he felt cheated. He felt guilty too, because of Natalie, but he couldn't understand how he hadn't seen this girl before, and couldn't help but feel bereaved, even though he hadn't known her.

He wondered what her name was, what she'd been like, and he knew she was dead but some crazy part of his brain was imagining what kind of couple they would have made. It was the shock he supposed, the first time he'd seen a dead person, but she *was* beautiful.

It was disturbing too that her face looked so serene and undamaged. He glanced again at the mess of blood, then back to the alabaster white of her face, the soft red of her mouth. He reached out and rested his fingers on her lips, still warm, a warmth that upset him, and then something moved and he jolted back in shock. He didn't know what the movement had been but he looked again at her face and saw now that her eyes were open. He edged closer and looked into them. Maybe it was just a reflex reaction – but no, they were moving.

She was looking at him. He didn't know whether she could actually see him, whether or not she was registering anything at all, but she was looking at him. He didn't know what to do. He couldn't understand how someone with her head caved in like that could still be alive.

Her lips moved as if she was trying to speak but they hardly separated and no sound came out, just a few small delicate bubbles of blood stacking up on top of each other at the corner of her mouth. She wasn't dead but he didn't know what to do. And it was worse because he knew she had to be close to death.

Her head was caved in and there was blood coming out of her mouth. She was looking at him, trying to speak, and she was dying and he didn't know what to do. He knew he was meant to comfort her or call for help but he'd never been this close to death before, had never been close to death at all, and he was scared.

He could feel the panic building, firing up in his muscles, urging him to run, to get away from her. He tried to tell himself to stay calm but she was dying right there in front of him and the two of them were alone in the road and he didn't know how to reach her or how to help. He was just scared, like a child, wanting someone responsible to take it away from him.

He was walking before he knew it, walking away, and the voice was screaming in his head to go back. She's still alive, he yelled to himself, she's still alive, do something, go back, but he couldn't go back. He kept walking along the road and he ignored his own internal screaming and told himself that it was too late to walk back anyway, because she'd already be dead.

He should have stayed through those final moments and he hadn't but she was dead, she had to be. Her head was smashed in, she'd been thrown fifty feet, maybe more. She was dead. He kept telling himself and he knew it wasn't true and he kept screaming inside his own thoughts but he couldn't go back. He couldn't.

The car was up ahead, passenger door open, tail lights, exhaust trailing, the vague silhouettes of the four people inside. He realized he was crying, not sobbing but with tears flooding down his cheeks. He wiped them away with his hands, then with the cuffs of his coat. He didn't want the others to see him like that. He had to stay calm.

He breathed deeply as he got closer, and when he got to the car he kept his head facing into the road until he'd closed the door and the light had gone out. He was feeling more in control now, and focused on the air of expectancy that was coming from the four of them.

'Go,' said Alex, looking at Matt.

'Shit,' said Rob, not needing to hear any more.

Matt looked amazed and said, 'She's dead?'

Alex nodded, another round of expletives from the back, Matt's face a blank.

'What about the car?'

Matt shook his head. 'Not a scratch. I couldn't even see where she hit. You're sure she's dead?'

Alex nodded again and said, 'She must have been thrown about fifty feet. Her head's all smashed in.'

Matt looked at Alex as if reminding him of something basic that he'd forgotten, and said then, 'Well, we can't just leave her there.'

'We have to, Matt. You've had a drink. If the car was damaged maybe. Look, just go; we need to get somewhere we can discuss this without being seen.' What he really wanted was to get away from what he'd just seen back there, from the confusion of feelings and guilt, from the fear.

'Matt, just go,' said Natalie, sounding sober now, frantic. It was almost as if she'd picked up on what was going through Alex's mind.

Matt still looked uneasy but pulled away, driving into the centre of town with them all in silence. Alex wished somebody would speak but nobody did. All he could hear was his own silent prosecution, throwing the accusations at him, that he'd abandoned her while she was still alive, that he was a coward, that he could have saved her but had run scared.

Matt drove through town and out towards the quay road and then the silence was broken as Will said, 'I'm gonna be sick. Matt, I'm gonna be sick.'

He swung the car into one of the empty spaces overlooking the river and Will scrambled out, running to the railing and hitting it with so much force it looked like he might go over and into the water. They watched him in silence for a while.

Then Matt turned to Alex and said, 'There's no damage at all to the car, nothing.'

Alex nodded but didn't say anything and they continued to watch Will. After about five minutes Natalie said, 'You think we should see if he's okay?' Alex misheard at first, a guilty twitch of muscle at the thought that she was talking about the girl, the girl he'd left to die in the road. She was as good as dead already, he was convinced of that. But that didn't excuse anything. He could have stayed with her, and he didn't know what her real chances had been; he wasn't a doctor.

Maybe she was still alive, lying there in the road wondering why he hadn't come back. For all he knew, the damage to the back of her head had looked worse than it was, and people survived the most appalling injuries. He had a fleeting image of her in hospital, Alex visiting, getting to know her as she recovered. He shut it down quickly though – she was dead.

'I should go to the police,' Matt said and Rob and Natalie started to discuss it but he couldn't concentrate on what they were saying.

His mind was on the other side of town. Whether she was dead or not she was lying in the cold and dark in the middle of the road over there, a red shining halo on the tarmac around her head. She'd been beautiful, a human being, and he'd left her in the road like some wild animal.

And he'd left her there still alive. What had she been thinking as she'd looked up at him, that he might help her, that he'd stay with her? Surely that was the least she could have expected, the minimum amount of human compassion, and still he'd fallen short.

He was ashamed of himself and yet still scared. Even now, telling himself she couldn't still be alive, he was too afraid to suggest going back. And he couldn't rid himself of the look of her eyes on his face, desperate and alone. Why couldn't he have stayed with her? Why couldn't he have stayed calm? He'd killed her.

'Alex?'

'She's dead.' The words came out without him realizing what he'd said, unsure even what he was responding to. It seemed to be the right answer though, Rob and Matt using it to continue their discussion.

They were talking about whether or not to go to the police. Alex tried to think about it rationally. He tried to think of it from their respective points of view, seeing immediately that it would be bad news for Matt, those drinks working against him. And it hadn't been Matt's fault; she'd run in front of the car.

For the other four and for Matt especially it was probably better not to go to the police. For his part, he felt like it didn't matter. For the first time in his life he'd been tested and he'd failed. He'd left her to die in the road and it didn't matter if they went to the police or not.

Nothing he did would ever remove those moments from his mind: her face, her pleading eyes, that sickly smell of peach schnapps in the cold air. Nothing would ever remove the shame of his cowardice. He'd let her die alone, was letting her die as he sat there, and for that weakness he'd be damned for ever.

His only hope perhaps, even now, was to tell them to go back. And through all his confusion, through the storm of voices, he knew that was what he had to do, tell them to go back, call the police, do everything possible, because if he didn't, he would never forgive himself. And he would never rest again.